THEM

S.SESHADRI

Contents

Disclaimer

This is a work of fiction. All characters in the book are fictional and imaginary. Any similarity with any person, living or dead, is purely coincidental.

Preface

I love this question: *Why do people believe in ghosts?*

Spirits and various supernatural entities form an integral part of the socio-cultural beliefs of all religions in our country and occupy an important place in the Indian culture. Belief in 'Bhoot' (ghost) has been deep-rooted in the minds of the people of India for generations.

Cultures worldwide believe in ghosts that survive death and live in another realm.

Usually, a paranormal story wouldn't catch my attention. Then 2020 happened. Covid-19 happened. Lockdown happened. The Covid-19 pandemic had wholly turned the world topsy turvy.

Reports of paranormal activity increased during the coronavirus pandemic. I heard weird stories about people experiencing strange, unexplained sights or sounds. Quarantine life at the time of the coronavirus pandemic was giving a variety of experiences to people.

I found writing short stories more challenging than writing lengthy stories. Within a few pages, I had to clarify what I wanted to express, a demanding job indeed. Every story locked in a small room of my brain manifested in written form.

I have based these stories on India, the land of mysteries. These paranormal incidents, phenomena, and happenings probably have no explanations whatsoever.

Horror is a peculiar genre. I have kept an eye on diversity. Some people say that ghosts definitely or probably exist! Believe it or not!

The twelve diverse, ultra-creepy stories are probably meant for you if you look for chills down your spine. They will intrigue and delight you in equal measure.

Stranger at the Door

The villagers thought that the old woman had one foot in the grave.

Her face was more wrinkled than a crumpled piece of parchment paper. But people had noticed that her mind was sharp, and her skin had no connection with the thing between her ears. She looked ninety in a photograph taken at a local photo studio a decade ago!

The old woman's age was beyond the average life span, and her heart was beating stubbornly to keep the treasure chest safe from robbers, cheaters and charlatans, which were aplenty in the coastal town. But now, her gait was infirm with arthritic joints and failing eyesight.

So people wondered if she had a mask covering her face and wanted to pull away the veneer of age to see the person inside. But no one in the village dared to because they were gossiping in hush tones that she was the guardian of some kind of cursed booty her long-dead husband had left her. And anybody who dared venture into her house would never return.

The fishing village had sprung up near the seashore, inhabited mainly by fisher folk. It looked like it had no planning and great enthusiasm for architecture. Every house was different and was facing different directions.

It made the place as eerie as one could find. The ugly looking grey building, where the old woman lived, stood in the middle of an empty, abandoned mud road. No one went near it as one could sense the evil presence within it as it darkened up the road. People who perforce had to cross the street heard the floors creak as though some spirits were roaming inside the soulless house.

For years after the demise of her sailor husband, a window was the old woman's only connection to the outside world. She didn't have a telephone, and the door would open partially to let a home nurse or a grocer in as and when they called out to her from outside the gate. Without this human presence, the house would be as quiet as a mausoleum.

To scare away street urchins and other petty thieves, the old woman had placed human and animal skulls and bones all around the house. This weird collection frightened away the boys who came to taunt her or throw stones at her home. Or so they thought! Rocks hit some curious people who dared to sneak up to the house and peer through the dusty panes from nowhere. The news spread fast in the small town, and she was left alone to fend for herself.

• • •

It took him a day to reach the fishing village that had grown into a dense and cluttered place. The small buildings were different, borrowing this and that from another era. Many rickety shops had come up since he last visited, and there was a stone church right in the middle of the village. The village looked like an example of terrible planning with utter disregard for the basics of architecture.

Everything appeared beaten down and baked by the sun. The summer sun was everywhere: in the dust, in the fish spread all over large tracts of ground to dry, in the smells of spices and overripe fruits. The last time he had visited the village was when her partner, Nidhi Jacob, was alive. That was decades ago, and till recently, he was not aware of the rumours of the treasure chest in possession of his widow.

Selvam took everything, sentimental and valuable, on the black market. He planned a robbery born out of simple greed and malice, a form of revenge served on a platter of ice. It was always this way for him, love turning into hate, and in his warped way, he felt secure when it did. He grew up amidst evildoers, and he could understand what evil meant.

Violence was in his blood. Selvam found out everything about the old woman, every perceived flaw, every vulnerability, and he knew where to put the pressure. He considered the old woman to be a helpless, tottering soul trying to move around with the help of a walking stick. Strangely he felt sorry for the lonely, unpopular old woman whom the entire village had shunned. But then the treasure chest had occupied his mind day in and day out!

To a robber whose heart is in his profession, business is business. There were this lure and a challenge in this job. As pre-planned, he set out on a quiet day late in the day to prevent suspicions from the watchful villagers. But then, no one bothered him as they had more important things to think and plan than mere idle curiosity built on superstitions.

The sky became dark as he reached the old woman's house. He parked the nondescript hired car by the gate in front of the tall wall of the house for a quick, quiet and unostentatious departure.

He did not like how the moon shone down upon the skulls and bones placed in the branches of the gnarled trees.

He cursed himself for being superstitious. He had to concentrate on the job on hand than ponder on idle thoughts. He feared that it might be an unpleasant work to silence older women who are stubborn and perverse. But then, since she was ancient, he could quickly muffle her weak screams. He prided himself in his art of making unwilling persons voluble.

He slowly moved up to one lighted window and put his ear to the window pane. He heard the woman talking to herself as if she was in the middle of some game. At the last minute, he wondered whether the old man had died before revealing where he had hidden his treasure. A thorough search would be time-consuming. He decided to use force to get the exact location of the treasure chest. He traced his steps back and knocked on the weather-beaten wooden door.

In minutes the sky was dark once more as the clouds passed, and the moon appeared to be playing a game of hide-and-seek. Selvam could feel the heat, and then there came soft music, but the words eluded him.

The massive doors opened slightly inward. The woman at the door was so fragile that Selvam thought he would rupture her even with the softest of touches. Her open eyes were not focused but moved randomly, obscured with cataracts so entirely that he could not even guess her eye colour.

Her hair was wispy over a scalp that showed signs of pressure sores, pink from constant contact with a pillow or chair. The age spots gave her skin a coffee-stained look, and her jowls hung a good inch below the chin.

Selvam opened his mouth to begin to speak when the woman delivered a good strong poke in his stomach with her walking stick. Surprised by the sudden and unexpected aggressiveness, Selvam closed his mouth abruptly with a gasp. He quickly recovered from his shock and found his voice.

He called her name loudly.

"Mary, Mary, can you hear me? I am Doctor Selvam, a good friend of your late husband. I was overseas all these years, and as soon as I came to this village, I rushed to give you my condolences and pay my respects to my dear departed friend."

The man's white coat, a stethoscope adorning his neck, and the overall demeanour of a doctor must have impressed the old woman; she stepped back and let him in.

"My dear Mary, you don't look very well at all. Let me check you." Selvan pretended to examine her and talked to her in a friendly manner.

After getting no reaction from her, he asked her to raise her arms. Again there was no reaction. He applied mild pressure to her temple, and her hand moved feebly. She was still in there all right but appeared deaf and half-blind. 'This makes things easier for me to bump her off,' he thought to himself.

"Welcome to my home," she said feebly and gave him toothless smile, "and to yours. I'm so glad you chose to come and live with me for eternity." Selvam let his eyes roam the room for escape options, confused with her utterance. Worn-out carpets partially covered the floors that had gathered dust; the walls were just bricks behind the fallen plaster.

Then as the old woman turned and took two steps, her legs wobbled. Selvam lurched forward and held her frail body tightly, preventing her from falling.

"That was very nice of you," the old woman said. "What brings you here? Hope you are not one of those mean villagers."

Selvan laughed. "No. Not at all, Mary. I told you I am a doctor and a good friend of your husband. I have come here to meet with you and offer my heartfelt condolences."

The old woman asked him to follow her to the centre of the big hall. There was the front door, the window and whatever odd things and pieces of furniture lay behind her in the kitchen. Selvam followed her, keenly observing the interiors. He noticed a short flight of stairs leading to the top floor. There was a table in the centre of the hall with two wooden chairs placed opposite each other.

The old woman motioned him to sit on the one facing her and back to the door.

Selvam sat opposite the old lady, who was smiling at him; she then took out a pack of playing cards. He felt vaguely uncomfortable as he felt the piercing look of her colourless eyes. Intuitively he felt something scary creeping up his spine and started looking out of the corners of his eyes for an escape route. Maybe he could make a plan without being detected.

The old woman shuffled the deck and dealt the cards. "This is my favourite part," she said as if they were watching some soap opera on TV. Selvam saw her arms become free, and she raised the pack of cards with a trembling hand up to her face.

"Take a card," she said. His hand obeyed without conscious thought, turning over the King of Spades. The old woman opened her mouth, but instead of the giggling coming from her, it radiated from the walls. "The King of Spade dies," the voices said. Selvam was stunned. He looked around, trying to trace the source of the ominous sounds.

"Don't worry, and I'll bring you back for the next hand, "the old woman said coyly. It was the King of Diamonds this time. Selvam watched her with his mouth open, and this time the screams came out louder and more assertive.

"Ignore those sounds," Mary said casually. "Now, I want to tell you a story about my life and what made me live so long. I am sure you will give your life to hear it." Selvam held his breath and sat straight. "I am all ears," he said.

• • •

That was a Sunday, three decades ago. The dark grey sky restlessly grumbled. Mary was running around trying to close the windows of her large house. She was expecting her husband, Nidhi, at any time. She prayed at the small altar of Jesus Christ she had lovingly made with the best-carved rosewood. The thick black clouds struggled to withstand the burden of the weight the rain held and soon gave in. The rain poured down over the coastal village with a roar. Above the boom of the thunder, Mary heard the sound of loud knocks on the front wooden door.

Apprehending an attack by a thief, she peered through the keyhole and found her husband Nidhi Jacob standing at the doorstep drenched in the rain carrying a huge metal box on his head. She quickly slid open the latch and removed the chain to let him in.

Nidhi Pinto appeared to be afraid and in a hurry. He asked her to give him a hand to carry the box upstairs. After they moved the box upstairs, Nidhi told Mary that the large box was entangled in the fishing net hidden amongst scores of fish. He had assured his partner he would take it home and find out what it contained. He laughed it off, saying maybe it contained some pirate's discarded old clothes and other such junk.

The box was a sort of laundry trunk, yet it looked as if it belonged to a seafaring pirate. When they broke open the box, they were mesmerized by the contents that someone had carefully packed in it. There were gold jewellery, silver, and diamond necklaces, the cost of which they couldn't fathom. Nidhi told Mary to hide it in a safe place. He promised her they would leave the village to a distant land the following night and lead a luxurious life forever.

The following day when Mary was in the kitchen busy preparing her husband's favourite lunch, she heard voices upstairs. She listened to a man's voice, talking loudly to her husband. She couldn't make out what they were arguing. But the argument soon grew from nowhere into a tornado.

Fear is felt in the mind, but it also causes a powerful physical reaction in the body. Mary's dread was prompted by the phrases they were using. Then she heard what sounded like a fist fight going on. She had never known Nidhi to use harsh words or his fists. Suddenly she heard her husband screaming in pain. Recovering from a momentary shock, she rushed upstairs.

She saw her husband's body lying in the middle of the room to her utter horror. His clothes were blood-stained and ripped in several places. The knife had met flesh, soft and plump, as the tip of the blade sank deep enough to make Nidhi scream. She looked around in fear and found no one.

Then she heard a man jumping out of the window. She rushed to see who it was. But he was running with his face covered with a mask, got onto his bike, revved it up and was gone in seconds. She rushed to the place in the room where they had hidden the treasure chest.

It was safe. The stranger thought that Nidhi was dead before he could extract the information. He heard footsteps of Mary as she started climbing up the wooden stairs and immediately fled the scene.

The searches made by the police to capture the killer went in vain. The entire village forgot about Nidhi sooner than expected. Mary was crestfallen.

• • •

The old lady paused and took a sip of water and cleared her throat. After a moment, she started talking.

"It wasn't the day I had planned; a movie and dinner with Nidhi. But at least he left with words of love in the hour he spent with me after coming home. As my rage and grief subsided, his words healed my mental wounds; his thoughts calmed me as I loved my husband so much."

"I am touched to hear the tragic story, Mary. You must have gone through hell. But why didn't you take the treasure, move to a city, get married again and live in peace."

"Only ordinary people who have no feelings would think of doing that, Doctor Selvam," she said. "But I am made of sterner stuff. One feeling always remained burning in my heart which has kept me alive all these hellish years."

"Really? And what it may be, may I ask?" Selvam prodded her.

"Revenge." The old woman almost shouted, bending forward, taking Selvam by surprise. "The need for revenge was like a wretch gnawing at my soul, relentless, unceasing. My need for revenge was like a septic wound, and the only effective antibiotic was cold hard revenge. Savage. Spiteful. Unforgiving. So I decided to wait."

"Wait for what? For whom," Selvam asked.

"Of course, for the killer to return, you stupid man. I was sure the killer knew my husband and knew he had the treasure hidden somewhere in the house. He would surely return one day when things cooled down. I intuitively knew he would disguise himself and try to gain my confidence. I also knew he would spare no effort to kill me and escape with the loot. So, Jacob, am I making sense to you?"

Selvam jumped from his seat out of the shock of hearing his original name.

"Yes. That was the last word uttered by my husband before he breathed his last. Jacob... I am now going to settle old scores."

Selvam felt the panic begin like a cluster of firecrackers in his abdomen. Tension grew in his face and limbs. His breathing became more rapid, shallower. He ran about the room, searching for an exit. There was a trap door he hadn't seen before. He forcefully slid back the bolt and ran downwards, almost falling in his hurry.

An old woman's figure stepped forward from the shadows, hunched beneath a cloak. From the dark folds of the blanket, a withered brown hand, clasping a walking stick, extended; the long silver hair hung on her head, obscuring every part of her face.

As she approached, Selvam heard her talking – talking as if the conversation was two-way. He moved to the side. Then her face tilted up alarmingly, her features more heavily lined than a walnut. Her lips, stretched over toothless gums, moved. As she spoke, the words came out in rasps.

Selvam had not noticed the colour of the old woman's hair. They looked like that of wild animals and glowing. But he wasn't hallucinating.

"Stop!" she said, obstructing his path with her stick, "don't walk away in the middle of the game, Doctor! It's rude!"

Then he saw the stick had vicious-looking sharp blades embedded in it.

His scream was the kind of throttled cry that did not appear to be coming out of a human. It was a scream of someone in mortal terror. He was rooted to the spot and too afraid to run.

• • •

The word went around the village like an old steamroller, slowly and painfully. People reacted as if nothing had happened.

They cared about eating, sleep, and eating, so they had enough energy to work.

Some people talked about an unidentifiable body of a man washed ashore, horribly mangled with many cuts inflicted by sharp knives. The dead man appeared to be a doctor in a white coat with a stethoscope hanging around his neck.

Some people talked about an old car found in a trench after crashing against a culvert a few hundred feet from the old woman's house.

And some villagers spoke of hearing inhuman cries like that of a demon heard in the night.

• • •

The Padre of the church summoned the village elders and told them he found a treasure chest full of jewellery at the altar of Jesus Christ when he went to hold the mass one Sunday. He informed them that there was a scrawl on it saying 'For the Orphanage'. All of them shook their head in disbelief and quietly dispersed. But many villages dismissed it as village gossip.

But the old woman paid no attention to those idle gossips.

After all, she was ancient, feeble and reserved.

Harmless.

The End

The Wings

Nandi Hills is a beautiful small hillock located 60 km from Bangalore, the silicon valley of India. When I started the ride, the feeling of fresh air on my face, empty roads and the beckoning of the unexplored destination filled my heart with excitement. Unfortunately, as I neared the Nandi Hills, the weather turned ominously hostile.

As I approached the habitable side of the Hills, I was stopped at a local police checkpoint, monitoring the flow of traffic. A policeman came over and asked where I was headed. I flashed my ID and told him I would like to see the ancient big house everyone was talking about.

The policeman came closer with his face slightly grimaced. "Sir, the local people swear this house is haunted. It is not a good idea to visit it even during the daytime. The villagers say no visitor has come out alive from that house. The present owners are in the city. And have brought in a court order prohibiting the general public from visiting it," The policeman was genuinely serious and pleaded with me to go back.

His words sent a chilling wave through my spine. But I didn't lose my cool. I gave him a broad reassuring smile. I flashed my ID as an investigative journalist. "Please do not worry. I know my responsibilities. I have come to investigate and present a true account of the happenings in that big house before the public. And will report to you on my way back."

The policeman shrugged. "I can't refuse under the circumstances. But please be careful. And in case of emergency, dial this unique 3-digit number for help." I thanked him and kick-started my bike.

I noticed the policeman conversing with several people nearby.

• • •

I drove up the steep Nandi Hill roads. They were indeed narrow and curvy. For a newbie driver like me, it was a little scary. I wondered if it was wise to venture into this unknown territory.

But my chief editor's booming voice kept ringing in my ears. 'You have not given me a single report that will thrill my readers since I hired you a year ago. You are supposed to be an investigative journalist, but your reports turn out to be pedestrian, and I am losing my Sunday circulation. If you can't produce an engrossing story for the coming Sunday's edition, look for another job.'

While I was ruing my association with this weekly, my drinking buddies at the press tipped me about this location. "Look, man. You got to be successful in your profession and ready to take risks at the drop of a hat," Ramesh, a senior journalist, had said in all seriousness. I gave him a sceptical look and downed my beer.

"There is a dilapidated 100-year building atop a small hillock in Nandi Hills that is deserted for decades for unknown reasons. The locals swear that no one has entered the old house for ages, and they were afraid to go near it. They strongly feel that certain strange things keep happening in the big house like someone was lurking around."

"Oh! Really? I was not aware of it. I will talk to the present owners about it," I replied matter-of-factly.

"Don't you ever do it if you want a story?" Ramesh warned me. "The present-day young owner is a nasty lawyer and may bring in court cases against you for unlawful trespassing and for spreading rumours."

I ruminated on the possibilities for some time. Just before we dispersed, Ramesh gave a big slap on my back. "Just go there unannounced and find out the so-called paranormal phenomenon and create a thrilling account around it to please the editor. You owe me a beer on your return." He winked with an evil grin spreading across his face.

• • •

Sometimes we are called upon to take the road not travelled as a sort of scout, checking its safety, ensuring that it leads to some place of greater interest than to stick to well-known routes. I undertook such exploration with a degree of courage, a lot of faith, and a complete determination to uncover the story in the place. Riding through the hills is a delightful experience. However, it is always trickier and more dangerous than riding on open, wide highways. Those who love riding would tell you that the best way of enjoying two wheels is to make them carve their path through some inviting twists in the hills. Visibility is critical in the hills due to the narrow, primarily undivided roads. I got going with renewed enthusiasm. I felt some unknown force was beckoning me.

The mud road lay over the earth for as long as anyone could remember, and with no one to maintain it, it was for nature to reclaim in her own good time – and she had started in earnest. In the weathered cracks was gathered new soil, enough to tempt seeds to grow. Their roots grew in, leaving a bright green over the grey and the land was breathing, healing the old scars. When my soles met that road, I felt fire igniting within regardless of the challenge. I decided to walk this road to make discoveries that would bring passion and fire into my writing. I parked my bike under a banyan tree and walked towards the old house up the hillock.

• • •

In the middle of a sea of change, the old house was a relic from the past. It grew from the ground as an ancient seed of the mountain born to blossom. It had brought the perspective of passing years into a world that had accelerated beyond sense. No one appeared to be living anywhere near it. I climbed the steep hillock and grappled with a queer feeling of unease. Faceless stone statues flanked the archway, their features worn smooth by wind and rain. The path to my right led down the hill, and ahead of me stood the 'Gowda's Doddamane' (meaning the Gowda Manor), named after the family name of the original owners.

The 'Gowda's Doddamane' had been abandoned for over a century. Or so I had heard. The only modern-day building on this part of Nandi Hills was several miles away, a nursing home for ailing and ageing locals. The breeze tickled my hair from the back of my neck. I hugged my jacket tighter around me and walked straight. I could not place the source of my discomfort. I had spent much time inside crumbling buildings in my two decades of investigative journalism. Perhaps it was the undefined giant trees that grew alongside the path that looked grotesque. Maybe I could sense they did not belong here.

The crumbling manor loomed larger as I approached. It was made of a brick and mortar stucco that looked out of place in the sylvan surroundings. It looked tired, with peeling lime washes and sinking edges, but, strangely, all the windows were intact. It looked like the house had become aware of itself, of the history that echoed within the walls. All the windows were closed as if the cold wind would make it shiver. I thought the old house did shut every door and window, darkly shrunken from the world, hoping to be invisible to the prying eyes. The path to the old house looked as if no one was using them, the mortar holding back the weeds that had overtaken the neighbouring ways with ease.

Suddenly the sun came out from behind the dark clouds, bathing the old house in gentle sunlight. I could see the giant front door was made of dark rosewood. It was off its hinges and a shiny knocker dangled with gravity. The steps leading to the front door were old, uneven and slippery due to the recent rain. I grabbed the rusty rail with my free hand and moved up gingerly. I took a stone and cast it through the broken window, just to startle anyone in there. Nothing happened. I guess it was empty after all. I pushed on the door expecting it to swing open, but it did not. Now that was interesting and didn't bode well. I stepped back and took a detour of the old house. I touched each brick and felt the texture that had greeted intense summers and hail storms with such dignity. It was sporting a shiny new coat of moss. I presumed history lived here with the ghouls and ghosts. Haunted places make good stories. They don't scare me. How can I be scared of the dead when the living is so volatile?

• • •

I took a step back and saw cracks in the walls everywhere, with wild plants pushing through the cracks. The lacework of the spiders stretched out between timber frames of the porch, freely moving together in every welcome summer breeze. And then I noticed something unusual.

Sitting on the nearby trees and crumbling compound walls were several crows. Silent and looking restless and expectant. They were not making any noise and hadn't attracted my attention earlier. Some had gathered on the unkempt lawn on the rear side of the old house. More crows with perfect black inky wings alighted upon a nearby branch.

Intrigued by the strange and quiet scene unfolding before me, I looked at the walls and found various shapes of worms pushing their way up through cracks in the wall. But the family of crows just sat there fluttering their black wings. Surprisingly, they did not care to look at the worms on the wall or those that crawled out of the foundation. They appeared to be patiently waiting for a bigger meal. I recalled my grandmother's voice.

'Crows may be ugly, but they are special. They carry souls of the dead.'

'But, Grandma, what happens when a bird gets trapped inside a house?' I had asked her.

'Then the soul is trapped too. Why do you think so many houses are haunted?'

A crow fluttered upwards, drifted past above my head and landed on the sill of the second-story window. Startled by the sudden movement, I ducked and then looked up. A woman's wrinkled face peered from the window, watching me from a room I thought was empty. I raised my hand in greeting when solid bony fingers wrapped around my wrist and whipped me around.

An ancient-looking woman, who appeared to be from the past, dragged my face close to hers. Her breath was sharp and smelly. "Don't let me die here," she cried, her eyes boring into mine as if she could burrow her thoughts into my head by the force of her stare. Her rheumy eyes filled with tears.

"Don't let me die here," she repeated and started crying loudly as two men in traditional eighteenth-century warrior dress suddenly appeared by her side to pry her clenched fingers from my arm. "Come back before we hurt you," one of the men reprimanded loudly. He led the old woman away, patting her back and murmuring in a strange language in soothing tones. The taller one with a huge moustache remained and fussed over my wrist.

"I'm sorry about the unfortunate incident. Did the old woman hurt you?"

"I'm fine," I assured him. "I apologize for trespassing. I hope I didn't disturb the good lady."

"No, no. Madam Gauri is... not well. Now let me check your wrist."

"If I may ask, why did she keep on repeating she didn't want to die here?"

The tall man shrugged and said scornfully. "The blabbering of dementia."

When he was satisfied that my arm and wrist were still in working order, the man with the moustache stepped back. "I'm supposed to tell you not to be so close to the house. I will permit you to walk around the estate like a special case. It's pretty this time of year. It's just that house is not structurally safe. But do not make any attempt to enter the house."

I nodded in acquiescence, looking at the crack spread from the house's base up the three floors.

The man with the moustache shivered. "This place gives me the shivers, "his voice dropped to a whisper. "Supposedly, in the past, some people living here tried to burn it down. The walls are crumbling. Someday the whole house will split open like an overripe carcass." He let out a loud laugh which shook me a bit. "I better get back before I get in more trouble," he grimaced. "Madame Gauri is old, but I swear, she's very troublesome."

I waved at him as he trudged towards the back door, which I had failed to notice. Before heading towards the front porch of the building, I looked again at the second-story window. It was empty.

'It doesn't matter,' I thought to myself. 'I will find out who lives here when I get in this haunted house.'

This adventure was not my first ghost encounter, nor my hundredth, yet that strange, foreboding feeling still clung to me as I hurried past the ominous-looking trees after collecting my tool kit and torch kept in my bike. I successfully forced opened the lock to the heavy front doors of the old house and slipped inside.

I found myself standing in the foyer; the walls' yellow-green colour was faintly visible. Dark clouds had covered the sun, making the afternoon lose its glow. I crept deeper into the house. It looked like someone had gutted it deliberately. The culprits had removed all the furniture and paintings. Ash blanketed every surface like layers of dust, and the air was stale and dry.

• • •

"Hello, Madam," I said softly to the woman at the top of the grand staircase, which I thought was Madame Gauri. "I'm here to set you free."

I would estimate she was in her seventies. She wore a worn-out ancient 'saree', the traditional Indian women's dress, and her platinum hair hung limp. The room was dark, but she had a pulsating glow. She was breathing hard. "Hello," I whispered again. "I'm here to free you if you can take me into your confidence." I picked my way across the dusty floors littered with odd items.

As I moved forward, my foot hit a hard object, and I pitched forward. I landed hard on my knees and grunted. I could feel the splintered edges of burnt wood rake against my ankle. I was sure it had drawn blood. Wincing, I gingerly raised myself and looked up. The woman had vanished. I sighed and continued towards the stairs in the dark. Cursing, I carefully prodded the floor thoroughly with my shoe before moving forward.

As I reached the banister, the woman suddenly showed up as she had disappeared. "Show me where your room is. I will carry your stuff," I said. The women spun and walked down a hallway. I followed.

She reached the second floor, opened the door on the left and passed through it. I caught up and twisted the doorknob. The door swung inward, and I entered.

Aside from a few oddities and an unkempt bed, the room was empty. I limped to the window. I could see the spot on which I stood this afternoon. I peeped through the dirty window glass pane, trying to find any unusual activity outside. There were no crows outside. I could partially open the window to survey the area. I was surprised to find not a single bird anywhere in the vicinity. I leaned against a wall and massaged my knees.

"Where are the crows?" I called out.

She appeared next to the fireplace and extended a finger. I frowned. "I have already noticed the fireplace," I told her. She stamped a scrawny leg, making no sound but disturbing the dust. She jabbed her finger insistently. I limped towards the fireplace and followed the line of her arm to an ancient-looking wall-to-wall wooden closet.

The wood felt rough as I ran my fingers back and forth the shutters to find the knob to open it.

I looked at the woman. She was across the room now, near the window, with her head cocked to one side. I gripped my hand around the knob attached to the closet and pulled the hinged door.

I staggered back a few feet, shocked from deep inside.

Inside were several dead crows. I couldn't imagine how they got there.

'*Not caught,*' I thought. '*Entombed.*' I turned towards the old woman. "These are your birds?"

She nodded, her eyes big and mournful. I wondered who she was and what had happened to her. She was looking harmless like a child, trapped alone in this comfortless house for a century. I offered her a smile.

"I will get this place cleared and set you free." Her timid smile met mine. I took a box from the recess, blew off a thick layer of dust, and then untied the twine. I was about to open the box when I saw the wings of the dead crows flutter. It was almost imperceptible, perhaps a mere trick of the light or my breath disturbing the corpses.

Then it shivered again.

The grotesque closet had been undisturbed for many, many years. And yet, the dead birds were inside.

My eyes slid sideways. I could see the old woman on the edge of my vision – her face. There was something about her face. Something... trembling, like her skin, was about to slip off.

I snapped my gaze to her. She looked normal, as normal as a ghost can look. Still...

"These are your birds?" My tone was soothing, loving. She nodded emphatically and started walking into the hallway, beckoning me to follow. I hesitated and then shone my flashlight on the closet.

The birds were grotesque and disfigured: their wings looked unnaturally stiff and shiny, body too long.

'*Are they crows?*' I wondered.

'*Crows, living or dead, are often symbolic. Some believe, if you see a dead crow, it means you're nearing the end of one phase in your life and moving into another.* 'I remembered my grandmother's words. '*It looks like I am going to get a better job.*' I smiled wryly to myself.

I had walked the grounds this afternoon. I would expect a place this old, with this much history, to be teeming with tethered spirits. And yet, I found only one.

A cold fist clenched around my heart. I turned off my flashlight. The old woman stood in the centre of the room. "Did you eat them?" I asked quietly. "The others?" She was trembling, struggling – her face wobbled.

Then she slumped. Her arms dropped. Dark spots bloomed on her face, spreading, taking the place of her eyes and her mouth. They were made of black liquid, of smoke, of nothing. Her eyes were gaping wounds of darkness, her mouth a black gap. It looked like she was bleeding shadows.

Her 'saree' wrapped around her shrivelled body started to drift towards me.

My heart battered against my ribs. '*It's a ghost, it floated through a door, it couldn't move a brick, No, it can't touch me. It can't touch me.*' I reassured myself.

But it did tug on my hand. I felt its fingers.

Flesh, it can touch.

My leg felt warm. I realized I was bleeding heavily from the injury.

I smiled at the creature and closed the closet. "All right, let me set you free."

I quickly made my way back down the hallway and began my descent down the staircase, slowly, slowly.

I held the box with its soul in one hand, and in the other was my flashlight. I could not set it free. I did not indicate that I wanted to flee, no indication.

It was beside me, in front of me, behind me. It appeared and vanished, circling me, assessing me.

Warm sweat was pouring down my entire body. I could not tell if my heart was racing or if it had stopped altogether.

Maybe, I could set the house on fire. I could get outside. Get outside without the box. I could hear it fluttering inside the box; it wanted to get out.

I smiled tenderly into the darkness. I knew it was watching me though it had no eyes.

"Let's set you free."

I latched the box shut, retied the twine.

The figure was suddenly in front of me. It touched my hand.

I blanched.

It knows it knows, it knows, it ...

I blinded it with the flashlight, shining the brightness at its grotesque face.

Nothing happened. It didn't vanish. It was not frightened by the light. It was toying with me, like a cat with a mouse.

I screamed and hurled the box into the depths of the dark house. I raced towards the gap in the doors, towards the tendrils of light peeking through, towards safety. My foot hit the edge of the hole in the floor. My heel dangled over nothing. I almost regained my balance.

Long, bony fingers wrapped around my ankle and yanked. I heard a snap. I crumpled. I tried to pull my leg from the hole, but I nearly passed out from the pain. My leg felt wet, and I knew I was bleeding profusely.

I screamed for help, screamed as loudly as I could.

I was dizzy. I tried to crawl towards the door, but the jagged pieces of wood trapped my leg.

My flashlight had rolled out of reach. The bulb flickered and went dead.

In the darkness, I heard the fluttering of wings surrounding me. They were all over me, toying and waiting for me to die. They only eat the dead.

Then I heard voices outside repeatedly shouting, "Who is inside?"

I tried to scream.

I heard footsteps coming closer and banging of sticks on the steps.

Someone was blowing a shrill whistle. The police had arrived.

I heaved a sigh of relief.

'*No crow will carry my soul to Heaven*', I thought to myself as tears of relief welled up in my eyes.

The End

Out of the World

Reports of paranormal activity had increased during the coronavirus pandemic. There were reports that some people experienced strange, unexplained sights or sounds. Quarantine life at the time of the pandemic was giving a variety of experiences to people.

The paranormal helpline started by 'The Paranormal Company' provided free assistance for spreading awareness against blind faith, superstitions, black magic, witchcraft, and overall supernatural understanding. A helpline number was set up by Jay Kumar, one of India's famous paranormal investigators.

The day he launched the helpline, Jay started getting a continuous flow of calls from people of all ages and sexes, who expressed fear and annoyance. When he investigated their cases, he found that binge-watching horror movies and series and listening to podcasts back-to-back were the reasons for causing concerns in their minds.

Jay was receiving over eight to ten calls daily on an average, out of which 90% of the cases were similar. People claimed to have seen a ghost, heard some unusual noise, or felt that someone was constantly watching them through the windows or from some dark corners.

"In several cases, I have found that persons claiming to experience any such unusual incidents had been reading horror books or binge-watching mystery movies. When my team of psychologists questioned them about their routine activities, family history, past trauma, we found out that many of them had created a fictional ghost in their mind," said Jay.

"We have investigated over one hundred haunted locations and closely studies over two hundred paranormal cases. Ever heard strange noises and household objects mysteriously move or are suddenly gone? How about levitating, whole torso vaporous apparitions, in the famous words of 'Ghostbusters'? Can one really believe such stories in the twenty-first century?"

"I'm a fairly rational person," said Mr Kumar, 30, who worked in an IT company. "I try to think what are could be the tangible things causing this? I check with others and search the internet to find out plausible reasons. But when I fail to get any reasonable answer, I start to wonder."

He was not alone. Jay organized a hundred other participants to share their experiences and solve this growing psychological trauma. Questions flew thick and fast. "Do you believe in ghosts? Why or why not?"

"Do you hear unfamiliar and unusual noises in the middle of the night?"

"Have you seen household objects mysteriously move?"

"How about free-floating, full-torso vaporous apparitions?"

Some of these people were frightened, of course. Others said they were amused.

Jay was frustrated. These discussions were taking him nowhere.

"In the dangerous pandemic times, you are physically confined and also psychologically cramped. Your world narrows. You're trapped at home, and you need human contact – it's comforting to think that there's a supernatural agent here with you."

"Do you agree?" he questioned the audience. "Are you aware of the reports that are frequently appearing on social media? Why do you think of paranormal activity during this time of quarantine and social distancing?"

The meeting ended on a chaotic note. Jay bid farewell to his audience and left in a hurry. It started raining heavily.

He swore under his breath at the untimely rains as he had to drive fifty miles to reach home.

Softly splashing water droplets hit the car windows as he drove onwards. The skies were overhung with a blanket of grey, so much so that he could barely tell the difference between the day and night. Jay watched raindrops race down to the windows.

Time and distance were all that mattered. Jay wasn't stopping for anything. Not in the least for the slight rain. His eyes stayed glued to the GPS display on his mobile, tracking their position while the world passed in a blur of lights. The pounding music over the music system muffled the hiss of the car tyres over the smooth cement road. Jay leaned over to turn it down. In that instant, he lost the opportunity to evade a recently broken-down car with its lights off. Even if Jay had been paying attention, he would have been hard-pressed to make the manoeuvre. He barely had time to make a manoeuvre to avoid the stationary car.

The car crashed into the central barrier and tumbled over and over before coming to a complete stop. The moment the car hit the trees, Jay assumed he was dead. Then he kept fading and waking and fading and waking! He could taste the coppery blood pooling in his mouth. Then the excruciating pain started as he felt the aching and cracks in his bones. The severe pain in his head was the only thing that kept him alive. That's when his body gave up.

Silence.

Many people still believe in superstitions. But modern science reveals the truths behind most superstitions with proper scientific explanations. But somehow, they couldn't succeed in removing superstitious beliefs in people's minds because they couldn't give reasonable answers to every ancient thought. Jay had lived his whole life telling people that things such as ghosts and aliens did not exist.

He always believed that the concepts were more psychological than scientific. His theory was that humans created the ideas to find comfort or a scapegoat. If a person is sad and missing his dear one, the butterfly that visits him brings him comfort. If a person faces sudden calamity in his life, it is easier to blame the unknown spirits than accept responsibility for his actions.

Jay was trying his best to explain to the believers of ghosts the fundamentals of parapsychology, the extrasensory perception (ESP). There were unexplainable things in this world, but one must know the whole circumstance, not just stories provided by someone who desperately wants to believe.

But Jay Kumar's opinion changed when he became a ghost; here, he was disproving his theory. He thought that someone had brainwashed him. Someone was trying to destroy his beliefs.

Crash! Boom! When it was raining heavily, Jay awoke as a ghost in the evening.

Some people have always said that the ones that become ghosts have unfinished business left on earth. Now that he joined the other side, he had to think differently. Jay thought he had much-unfinished business. Now, he had a new lesson to learn: 'How to be a Ghost.'

In the beginning, levitating was an enjoyable pastime. He could travel distances effortlessly. He could overhear gossip and enjoy the ghost conversations. In the beginning, Jay enjoyed the absence of human needs, such as food and rest. But soon enough, he got bored.

Travelling became boring because he didn't have a partner to share the experience with. He was finding himself craving human necessities. He missed the *masala dosas*, the burgers with French fries, and a nap.

'*What's the point of spending a lot of living years alone to find peace and dying to be alone?*' He thought wryly! '*Now, I'm the loneliest man that one can imagine.*' He rued his situation.

He decided to change the scene and make friends with people living in far-off lands he had never visited before. So he decided to travel to Kashmir. He chose the location due to low pollution and din and noise than any other state. Living in Kashmir should prove to be an exciting experience.

He was sure of meeting several ghosts there and making peace with them. They had a seminar organized in the heart of Srinagar, and a large number of spirits were expected to attend.

Although he had the advantage of invisibility and flight, he did have some restrictions on travelling. He was unable to travel during rush hour. The amount of friction in the air due to toxic emissions from factories and vehicle exhaust fumes would slow him and he risked becoming frozen in time for hours or sometimes even days.

So, he planned to make the trip to Kashmir early in the morning while the chaotic commuters were still asleep. He snooped into Google and found that weather did affect a ghost's travel. He checked the weather conditions and noted it would be a chilly day but happily clear.

He learned that chill weather didn't affect spirits. *One positive to being a ghost*, he smiled to himself.

For a moment, he wondered what to wear for the occasion. It dawned on him that there was no need to fret about what to wear. Also, this was the first party that he had ever felt comfortable with only bringing himself. He realized that they all would look the same!

The following day, Jay began his flight. He flew low to the ground to watch people and get entertained by the humans' weird activities during the long trip. To his utter astonishment, he arrived before he knew it.

He was soon surrounded and was overwhelmed by the number of ghosts present at the venue. The event organizers provided him with a unique name tag at the entrance carrying number 007. He floated around and circled, eavesdropping on the conversations of the ghosts.

Some conversations made him tremble with fear. 'OMG! These are terrorists', he whimpered and quickly floated away. Once again, he circled on the other end and made some small talk with a few, "How was your flight?"

"I'm glad I came, what a wonderful experience," and some such small talks.

A reverberating voice called for attention. The conversations went silent, "We are about to get started with the event of the evening, the 25th Annual Raffle." There were cheerful boos from the crowd. The absence of clapping felt strange. Jay was most excited despite the lack of sound since it was his first gala function.

The raffle's first item was a coupon that allowed a ghost to feel human sensations for only two hours. Jay wondered how he would spend those two hours. He would drink a beer, or maybe two or three. He would have sex but wondered how he would differentiate between male and female ghosts. He would eat the largest *masala dosa* followed by a cheeseburger—two of his perennial favourite foods.

The announcer let out a loud Boohoo which sounded like a drum-. No. 324 was the winner.

The next item was even better. A pair of invisible, ghost-friendly cell phones, fully loaded with a dozen music channels, YouTube, GPS. Jay had missed enjoying music. He was unable to play music now because he was constantly moving. I would like to have this set of headphones. But unluckily for him, No. 230 was chosen.

There were a few other uninteresting items that were awarded to the appropriate numbers. The host then took a small break before revealing the best thing of the evening. The ghosts were abuzz about the final item. They were discussing the best article from the previous year, an invisible SUV, fully loaded. Several spirits could travel together without worldly interruptions. Jay wondered how many ghosts could fit into one car. Maybe he could catch a ride back when the gala function was over.

"Ladies and Gentlemen, I am now going to reveal the long-awaited prize." The announcer boomed. Jay tried to clap but couldn't.

The announcer declared loudly, "The modern era of the industrial revolution with emerging and enabling technologies and systems such as 5G, AI, machine learning, Big Data, IoT, blockchain, cloud computing, virtual/augmented reality and cyber security is bringing drastic positive impact on improving the quality of life and experience. We ghosts are ahead of human technology. The winner of this prize will be sent back to the land of the living! That's right; this is your chance to be a human again!"

The boos almost drowned out the announcer completely. "And the winner is...number 007!"

Jay double-checked his number. He quickly floated to the stage to ecstatically accept his prize! He got another attempt at life just when he had started making friends in the ghost world.

• • •

The egg yolk sun poured through the cracks in the blind and awaited entrance into Jay's eyes. Still, in the clutches of the Ghost's party, he hesitantly tried to open his eyes.

The visions in sleep came and went in waves, clinging on to the very last memory of the party but with little success. Patients in comas may benefit from the familiar voices of loved ones, which may help awaken the unconscious brain and speed up recovery. Jay had no idea why all of his loved ones were gathered around him, and he just thought it was a big party. In reality, he was gradually coming out of a deep coma.

Jay had made a full recovery and appeared utterly unaffected by the coma. He awoke to find himself not in his cosy bed or even in the protection of his home. Upon waking, Jay burrowed himself into the warm, soft sheets. He blinked away a kind of fogginess from his eyes and gazed out at the horizon; its vivid light extended across a rosy sky.

"I'll come to visit you tomorrow. Sleep well, darling." Jay recognized his wife's soothing and soft voice. "We are thrilled you have come out of the coma in quick time. We have to leave the ICU now. The craniotomy used to treat severe head injuries was 100% successful."

The doctor came back, peered at a lot of emergency equipment at the bedside, and plunged a needle into Jay's sore place. When the doctor released the medicine, Jay was blessed with relief! All the pain appeared to have left. The nurse asked, "Are you okay?"

Jay winked and whispered, "I'm okay as okay gets."

The End

The Man in Tattoos

Mumbai clubs have a reputation of being highly energetic places and Devil's Den was something one had to experience. The club was furnished with wooden decor and had a loaded bar with various alcoholic drinks and cocktails.

This most-frequented nightclub was located in the suburbs, glittering with rainbow lights and reverberating with the sort of beats that revved up the soul. The sound vibrations of the club energized the soul of the dancers on the floor and took them to a happier plane.

The mystery man moved towards the bar with a swagger. He was a man who surpassed the average male, macho with an attitude. It is the sexiest combination, the mark of a true alpha. The bar soaked in the ambience vibes. From the lazy spin of the fans to the flashing lights of disco lights, remote-controlled projector strobe lights.

"Who is the girl in red dancing alone to the tune, swinging sexily to the beat," he queried in a deep voice sipping his scotch the barman had placed in front of him.

"No idea about her real name," the barman said wryly. "The girl has no name because she exists in many realities."

She'd had so many names that none of them was 'hers'. The mystery man smiled at him. "Watch now," he said mischievously, winking at the barman.

Some folks wear a smile, and this guy was the smile. Everything about him was a soft and understated joy as he ambled across the dance floor and tapped on the shoulder of the girl in the red dress. She spun back angrily.

"May I offer you a drink of your choice?" he asked, smiling politely. The girl in red looked at his mesmerizing eyes, her head sizing him up. As he picked up the glasses, he felt her melting her body to his from behind, and he knew it was going to be a night to remember. He led her and wound his way through the warm bodies to order a drink at the bar.

"Call me Subhahu," he said gently. "What do I call you tonight?"

"Zeenat," she smiled coyly, "I was named after yesteryear's famous film actor."

Situated close to the Devil's Den, strategically built on the beach, Jim's Cottage offered air-conditioned accommodation and modern facilities throughout the property. It was quiet, and the rooms were made soundproof for privacy.

"Zeenat means beauty in Arabic. I find your name, Subhahu, very unusual. What does it mean?" Zeenat asked as soon as they entered the room.

He glared at her for a moment and theatrically tilted his head. "My parents named me after a mythological character. Subhahu was the son of Taraka."

Zeenat frowned and queried, "Who was Taraka? May I know?"

Subhahu kept staring at her. "In ancient Indian mythology, Taraka is an evil spirit or devil, especially one thought to possess a person or act as a tormentor in hell. She is a large humanoid creature. And so, Subhahu happens to be a Rakshasa."

Zeenat knitted her eyebrows in concentration, trying to recollect the stories she had heard in her younger days.

"Rakshasas are demons, and they are evil." Subhahu continued, "they are cold and indifferent."

Before Zeenat could react, Subhahu quickly removed his buttoned-down shiny shirt and stood in front of her, legs spread wide and hands on his waist, his broad well-toned, clean-shaven chest.

Zeenat gasped and flopped on the bed. On Subhahu's chest was a fright-inducing face of a Rakshasa tattooed in red and black and yellow colours. It looked like a design made by puncturing the skin with needles and injecting ink, dyes, and pigments into the deep layer of the skin.

The Rakshasa was fierce-looking, with two fangs protruding from the top of the mouth. He looked like a growling beast. And as an insatiable man-eater that could smell the scent of human flesh.

Suddenly, Subhahu's fingers were on Zeenat's red dress, tearing it apart. He caressed her bare skin with the broken and dirtied fingernails tracing her breasts. Zeenat saw in horror the physical transformation taking place in Subhahu's body. He let his touch linger there for some time and started sliding downwards.

"Why are you lying there like a dead pig' he growled.

As he came near Zeenat, the face of the Rakshasa started throbbing. The accumulation of fatty plaque inside the carotid arteries created a turbulent blood flow. There was a pulsating sound that Zeenat found deafening.

Her face contorted into a scream-like expression. Subhahu got up and covered his chest quickly, and the pulsating sound stopped. His eyes sparkled in merriment.

"Do you want to see more art hidden in interesting places?" he asked her sarcastically as he caught Zeenat staring at his crotch.

"Would you care for a drink?" she asked fearfully, looking at his bloodshot eyes. For a moment, she thought that the liquor had played tricks with her vision. She moved away from him slowly but cautiously and poured him a stiff drink of Johnnie Walker Scotch whisky.

Subhahu grabbed the glass and quickly downed it in one hard gulp, gagging a little as he swallowed. A few drops of the fine liquor came dribbling down his chin. She smiled at him, took out a silk handkerchief, and gently wiped his lips.

"Are you an artist?" he looked at her questioningly. "Do you work in films?"

Zeenat smiled. "Yes. But I don't get plum roles frequently, and so I resort to the world's oldest profession to make some money on the side."

He smiled back in a patronizing way. "It doesn't sound like you have gone far in both your professions."

She didn't seem to mind the barb. She smiled back. "I get by, somehow." She could sense that he was already losing interest in the conversation. He poured another stiff drink, and once again, gulped it down disdainfully. But this time, before Zeenat could reach for the fancy handkerchief; he wiped his mouth on his shoulder sleeves and kept staring at her.

He got up and stumbled across the room, knocking down a chair as he moved to the dressing mirror. He kept staring at his face and then removed his shirt yet again, revealing the scary tattoo of the Rakshasa.

"Zeeni Baby," he purred, "I save mine and my friend's energy for special nights like this." He quickly moved towards the bed where Zeenat was sitting and flopped next to her. He wrapped his hand around her waist and gave her a tight squeeze till she winced in pain.

"I'm so glad you have a friendly disposition, Zeenat. I'm sure we are going to have a gala time."

Zeenat looked at his tattoo fearfully. It had started emanating heat. Suddenly, the pulsating sound became louder and quicker. Zeenat started to scream. "Shut your mouth, you bitch," she heard the Rakshasa snapping at her.

"Girls are living in other rooms. Please leave me and go to any of them," Zeenat begged.

He shook his head and took a long swig from the whisky bottle he was holding in his hand, which had turned into an animal's paw.

"I will pay you handsomely. Much more than what you earn in a day in your films," he said smugly.

His words started slurring. "NO!" Zeenat started crying.

"I beg you to leave me," she started getting up. Subhahu stared at her dumbfounded, repeatedly blinking as if in a state of confusion. "How dare you reject my generous offer?" He yanked her back onto the bed.

He moved in close, so the Rakshasa's tattoo was opposite her face. Suddenly, Zeenat felt nauseated by the smell of rotten flesh.

"You're not leaving till we finish the work," Rakshasa was growling.

He pinned Zeenat under him within moments. The Rakshasa's serrated blade-like tongue shot out and crawled into Zeenat's ear like a reptile.

"Let me go! Let me go," Zeenat tried to scream, pushing him weakly and trying to escape from the Rakshasa.

Subhahu had suddenly turned into a Rakshasa and was blistering and smouldering as if on fire. "No more wasting time. Let's get it over with," he whispered menacingly.

Zeenat gaped at his face, her mouth opening and closing soundlessly and gasping for air.

She pushed the demon with all her might in desperation. The monster jolted away in shock and fell off the bed in a befuddled heap.

He threw back his head and let out a strange-sounding roar. When a person is demonically possessed, they suffer from a diabolical being's complete seizure of their personality. This transformation allows the demon to dominate their person, allowing them to become, even somewhat physically, that demonic being.

Rakshasa thrust both his hands and reached for her. Zeenat recoiled from it and turned away from him. To her added horror; she noticed his fingers curling into claws, narrow and arched structure curving downward from the end.

She backed away from him, recoiling. He pressed the sharp claw on her neck, but only to lightly nick her and let a few drops of blood trickle down her throat.

"Who are you? Where did my friend Subhahu go?" Zeenat whispered.

The Rakshasa ignored her, and his red eyes hovered between her breasts and neck alternately. He then swung the claws at her chest without looking or aiming.

Her eyes widened in mute horror as blood bloomed from the laceration. She began to scream. Rakshasa clamped her mouth with a hairy palm to stop her from screaming.

"My master will be very upset if you scream. Don't scream. Nod your head once," Zeenat meekly nodded her head and the Rakshasa loosened his grip.

"Who are you?" she asked weakly between sobs. "Where is Subhahu?" she asked again amidst sobs.

"I am the real Subhahu, son of Taraka, the Rakshasi," the demon hissed, "I have the power to change my shape at will and appear as an animal, a monster, or even as a beautiful woman."

The Rakshasa paused and looked at Zeenat with eyes narrowed, dripping with spite. "Your friend was the physical manifestation of my soul. I used his body as a tool for experiencing the world, so the two are inextricably linked." His eyes glowed with savage fire.

"Your friend is resting inside me," Rakshasa grinned. "He will come out once I am done with you. I'm starving now." His venomous sneer turned into a wrathful grimace.

The piercing scream bypassed the ears but got muffled in the closed soundproof room. It was a scream of the mouth and lungs and a cry of the eyes and soul. The scream was primal. It had a raw intensity that told of urgency, of desperate need.

Subhahu didn't stop his car for a couple of miles. He pulled up near a dark lane and washed his face in the street's water tap. He wretched out the acid spray of liquor and blood. He wiped his face clean on his shirt sleeve and kept driving to the Film City at the other end of Mumbai, where a film shooting was in progress. He stopped under a giant banyan tree and changed his clothes.

"We are out of trouble, Rakshasa, my dear friend," he said sharply. He pulled some sweet-smelling gums from the glove compartment and started chewing them into the pulp. That would keep his mouth from stinking. He took out a bunch of lemon-scented sanitizer napkins and cleaned his hands.

"I cleaned up well after your sumptuous dinner, Rakshasa," Subhahu said wryly. He leaned back in his seat and closed his eyes. "I'm exhausted now, partner. Let me rest for a while now." He heard some sounds of grunting as his body reluctantly relaxed a bit. Rakshasa, who was clenched up and tensed, was slowly slackening. The pulsating beats quietened to regular heartbeats.

"Hey, have you come to pick me up?" the cheerful female voice woke him up. He slowly opened his eyes and saw a beautiful young woman leaning over the car window. He quickly gathered his wits and nodded his head.

"Great," the lady said. "I'm Maya, and as you may know, I am famous in the film industry. I just finished my shoot for the day."

"It's my honour to meet you, Ma'am," he said and got off the car and opened the door for her to get in. Suddenly, the wind opened his open unbuttoned shirt, and his tattoo of the Rakshasa was in full display under the moonlight.

"Wow! What a powerful tattoo! I love tattoos," exclaimed Maya, "I love the carving of black outlines, a minimal yet bold colour palette, and fearful tattoo imagery. It's awesome. Where did you get this done?"

"That's a long story," replied Subhahu with a mischievous smile on his face and with all the macho and sexy look in full display. "I will narrate it to you if you promise to offer me a drink at your place. You see, I have been waiting for you for hours, and I am parched."

"Sure thing," Maya said excitedly, "can't wait it hear it. What is the name of the tattoo?"

"I'll come to that. You said you like tattoos," Subhahu probed. "I don't see any tattoos on you."

"They aren't on display," Maya said, flipping her long mane and flashing upon him a coquettish smile.

"I'll show you once we reach my place," she winked. "It's special. I don't show it to anyone."

Inside Subhahu, Rakshasa was getting restless. His heart started beating faster, and his limbs began twitching, his breathing got heavy.

"Are you feeling all right?" Maya asked, her voice betraying concern and fear. You have started looking different.

"Stop talking bitch," Rakshasa growled. I am hungry, and I can swallow you whole now,"

"Hey, who was that talking to me?" Maya was visibly angry. "Let me get out of the car, and I'll show you who I am."

Subhahu was quiet. Uncomfortable at the sudden turn of events. He snapped his fingers and laughed. "You see, that was some play on the radio which made you nervous."

"That sucks," she said disdainfully. "Now start the car, and let's get the hell out of here. I thought you were sick suddenly."

"Yep," Subhahu intoned cheerfully. "Let's relax and talk about the tattoos." He looked back and asked, "Do I look like a sick man to you? Do you want to hear the story of my tattoo?"

He didn't look sick. He had such an energetic smile and such a vibe like he had the world in his hands.

"Sure thing," Maya said excitedly, "I can't wait it hear it. By the way, what does your tattoo signify?"

Subhahu looked at her with probing and piercing eyes. "It is a Rakshasa which means 'destroyer' or 'injurer' in the Indian language. The Rakshasa appears as a huge, misshapen human, having fiery red eyes and abnormally long tongues."

Subhahu turned to her and unbuttoned his shirt. "Can you see him properly now?" he asked.

Maya nodded in silence, her eyes betraying the fear swelling inside her.

Subhahu looked at her with probing and piercing eyes. "You see, Maya, the Rakshasas' eating habits are, in a single word, disgusting. They feed on human flesh and drink their blood. These monsters are shape-shifters, illusionists, and sorcerers. They eat human flesh and drink the blood and the life essence of an individual through this act."

"Why are you telling all this?" Maya almost screamed.

"Let me out of the car. I'm going to lodge a police complaint against you for molesting."

"Hey, stop screaming. Don't cry, darling." Subhahu cooed and stretched his arm as if to comfort her. The growling inside him became louder by the second.

Maya moved to a corner, shrinking at his sight and wrinkling her nose as the tattoo started coming alive and the wretched smell of the rotting flesh started overpowering her nostrils.

"Oh my God," Maya moaned. "Don't touch me. Who are you? What's your name?"

Subhahu looked at her, his eyes turning blood red and an evil grin spread across his face displaying the fangs.

"Rakshasa," he said.

The End

Helpline

The 'Sunset View Point' rests on one of the highest peaks of the Western Ghats on the Udupi-Agumbe Road. On a fine evening, with the setting sun come a sky of fire, the orange and the rich hues of red spreading its largesse across a grateful sky.

Agumbe lies in a hilly, wet region of the Western Ghats and is dotted with several waterfalls contributing to its breath-taking scenery. The Ghat roads are access routes into the mountainous Western and the Eastern Ghats – the mountain ranges of the Indian Subcontinent. These roads were built to connect to the hill stations established in the mountains.

As Arun Baliga swung the car to the lone Agumbe Ghat, his wife Deepti Baliga relished the roaring winds that twirled in her long hair and whistled in her ears. Memories of their honeymoon, journeying in a rickety bus to watch the glorious sunset in Agumbe, occupied her mind. That was twenty-five years, and Arun was starting his life from scratch. They hardly had any extra resources to spend on their honeymoon elsewhere. This was the closest point from the city of Mangalore, which was about a hundred kilometres away. They had come a long way from those humble beginnings.

Today, Arun was a prosperous businessman running a profitable seafood-exporting company in the city. That day was their twenty-fifth wedding anniversary, and they had decided to relive the memory of their first honey at Agumbe and watch the glorious sunset.

"You seem to have lost yourself taking in the beauty of the sunset, Arun," Deepti said in a soft voice while Arun kept gazing at the ever-changing colours of the sunset and didn't respond.

"Come on, Arun," Deepti prodded him. "It's time to hit the road as the shadows are closing in."

The silver-grey Mercedes cruised down the mountain, travelling towards Mangalore. Arun was in the driver's seat with so much soft leather around him that he could barely hear the 389 horsepower, 6-litre engine. At nearly a hundred kilometres per hour, the engine was only idling. But Arun didn't care to slow the mean machine. He wanted to feel the power of the car. It was a one hundred thousand dollars German engineering marvel, imported six months ago. One touch from the little finger and the Mercedes would leap forward. This was a car that sneered at speed limits.

Deepti fiddled with the remote control of the music system. She looked at Arun, smiled, and closed her eyes. She could feel the gentle rise and fall of the road beneath them.

From nowhere came the sound of a man's voice, loud and clear, so authentic that Deepti sat up straight. Arun too was taken aback and glanced nervously at the radio.

"This is the police helpline call, Sir. You have exceeded the speed limit – please slow down!"

"Who am I talking to? How can you tell I am overspeeding?" Arun queried haltingly.

"This is Inspector Francis Pinto, Sir," the polite voice continued in an authoritative tone. "We have our camera systems and equipment in place. Agumbe Ghat is the deadliest Ghat. It will throw you the most dangerous curves."

Arun held his breath, slowed down the car, and remained silent.

"I am glad you slowed down, Sir. Please drive carefully. I wish you a pleasant journey," the voice trailed off in a pleasant tone.

A heavy silence settled over them. Deepti shifted uncomfortably in her seat, and Arun wiped his sweaty palms. Both wondered how the Inspector traced them.

"I think I was a bit careless with my driving and went overboard with my driving skills. Sorry about that," he apologized to Deepti while throwing a furtive glance at her.

"Yes," Deepti agreed. "Let's be thankful to the Inspector for warning us. It is already dark, and I am a bit nervous about these Ghat sections."

She could not imagine what was in store for them. The thought of Kamya, their daughter, occupied her mind. She was missing her dearly. Deepti wondered how she was doing in her first year in medical college. She had promised to spend quality time with her over the weekends. She started humming with the music while Arun remained in a contemplative mood.

The sun sank lower, the light of day draining away, giving way to the velvety dark of night, and the air continued to cool. It soon became dark, and there was a deathly hush in the faint twilight. Gazing straight ahead, only half-aware of a world outside the claustrophobic comfort of the car, Arun's fingers stroked the wheel.

"What time do you see us reaching the city?" Deepti asked.

"We should make it in around 9 p.m."

"Good," she replied. "When we're close, I'll text Kamya and tell her we will reach her soon."

The late evening mountain air was rising now, and there was a headwind.

'At least it is keeping me in check,' Arun thought. He looked up the sky and noticed there was hardly a cloud in sight. 'Good, it would be a smooth drive all the way to the city of Mangalore.'

Suddenly it happened! THUD! THUD! The car lurched violently as unseen objects slammed into the windshield.

"Oh, my God!" Deepti screamed. Arun grabbed the wheel with both hands and fought to steady the lunging car.

Blood and parts of birds splattered on the glass, the engine sputtered, and the car pitched sideways. Arun fought for control as the road disappeared from view. Finally, the car hit the guard rails, slid downwards, and took with it a large piece of the rail down the slope. Luckily, on its way down, it hit a large tree and tottered to a stop.

"Arun, I'm hurt!" Deepti blurted out. Arun looked over and noticed blood running from her nose. She had hit her head against the front panel before the airbags inflated.

"Oh, no! Are you all right?" Arun reached across and touched her shoulder.

"I'll be okay, don't worry about me. What happened?"

"We hit a flock of birds on our climb." Arun groaned as he extricated himself from the airbag. "Thank God, the airbags inflated quickly, giving us a soft cushioning."

The engine began vibrating violently, and Arun cursed. "There appears to be serious damage to the car."

He reached forward and killed the engine. Silence. No sound now except for the whistling wind swept across them.

Deepti began gasping for air; she was in obvious pain. "Deepti...are you sure you're all right?"

"Yes, yes. I'll get the emergency kit and pack my nose. You call for help."

Arun quickly organized his thoughts. They were in danger, being totally enveloped by darkness over the rough Ghat terrain.

'Don't panic!' he told himself and desperately scanned the ground for a safe path up to the road.

The shadows were now twice as long. The air was cool, smelling faintly of a car's exhaust fumes. The sun had dipped completely, and the trees silhouetted against the darkening sky. Soon, their shadows melted away into the blackness of night.

Arun realized they were in serious trouble. There was no safe place anywhere to go. He grabbed up the cell phone and dialled the emergency traffic helpline number.

"Hello! Hello! Please help! I have met with a car accident."

There was no answer. He clicked again. "I repeat, Hello..."

"Hello, Sir. Please state your location," came a calm male voice.

Arun recognized the authoritative voice of Francis Pinto immediately.

"My name is Arun. My wife is with me. We are about twenty miles from the Agumbe Sunset point," Arun quickly answered.

"Are you hurt, Sir? How is your wife doing?"

"We are not seriously hurt, although we are in a state of shock. A flock of birds suddenly crashed into the windshield and made me lose control of the car."

"Okay, now listen. I'm near the Holy Family Church, approximately twenty kilometres from your position. Do you have GPS in the car?"

"Yes. But I think it is damaged due to the collision with a tree. I just have this cell phone with me, which has a

GPS. The standard app is used strictly for reference. I will need your step-by-step guidance."

"All right, Arun. We'll work on that. You must conserve the battery."

"Thank you. Can you let me know what I should do now?"

The radio was silent for a moment, and then the voice returned.

"Arun, climb up the slope and reach the main road. Are you sure you and your wife can walk?"

"That is a steep climb. You think we can make it?" Deepti butted in.

The male voice was still calm but concerned. "Hello. Whom am I talking to?"

"I'm Deepti. I am with my husband."

"Arun and Deepti, this is Francis Pinto again. I'm going to get you out of the problem. You stay calm. We're going to do this together."

The sudden change in conversation was disconcerting to Arun. He felt that Francis was not sure they could make it.

"What's he saying?" Deepti interrupted, obviously frightened. "I thought he would come and help us?"

"We're okay, and he seems confident. We'll make it."

But Arun knew it was almost impossible to get help quickly at this hour. He steadied his nerves as he put the thought away and focused on finding a path to the main road.

The voice came back on the line. "Look to your right. Do you see a large tree stump?"

"Yes."

"That's a good sign. Listen, there's a small path to your right, take that the path which will lead you to the main road."

"What's the man saying, Arun?" Deepti blurted out. "We should stay here till help reaches us?"

"Francis wants us to reach the main road, which will make us visible to any passing car. This guy appears to be knowing this Ghat section like the back of his hand."

Francis came back on the line as if he had overheard their conversation. "Deepti," he said, his voice reassuring. "I will get you out to safety. Do you have any children?"

The face of Deepti's daughter Kamya flashed into her mind. "Oh, yes, Kamya, she's eighteen and has joined the medical college. We're on our way to meet her."

"Deepti, I have a daughter too, her name's Mary; she lives not far from here. But don't worry, you'll see your daughter soon."

Somehow, Deepti's panic subsided. She felt assured, almost as if they were already on safe ground.

As the dark outline of distant mountains grew close, Arun could barely make out the line of small structures on the ground.

Arun clicked on the mic. "Francis, I think I can see the lights of a village at a distance."

"That's great. You're on the outer perimeter."

"Okay. A road will come up soon. It has street lights. Continue walking."

A police car red light suddenly appeared, the car's headlights lighting up the scene as it drew nearer.

"Are you all right?" the policeman inquired as he rushed over.

"We're fine, Officer," Arun replied. "But my wife does need some medical attention."

"No problem, I'll drive you to our local medic."

Deepti was being attended to for her injury at the small clinic. Arun sat nervously nearby. The policeman came and sat beside him.

"I am astonished," the man exclaimed. "That was the most incredible act you put on. How'd you do that?"

"What do you mean?" Arun queried with a bit of irritation.

"I mean, how did you manage to send a message to our control station, which is out of bounds from here? You managed to give me the exact coordinates."

"We were lucky for sure. It was the guy from the helpline– the traffic control station – who guided us. I didn't send any messages. Just followed his instructions."

"Control station?" the policeman replied incredulously. "What helpline?"

"The guy in the Helpline Control Station," Arun repeated.

"He talked to us and guided us to safety."

The Inspector put his hand on Arun's shoulder. "Sir, this control station has been closed for years. It's abandoned."

"But that's impossible," Arun exclaimed in disbelief. "It is situated next to the Holy Family Church. The guy talked to me all the way. He saved our lives."

"Who talked to you, Sir? What was this guy's name?"

"He said his name was Francis Pinto."

"But Francis Pinto died over 30 years ago."

"No," Arun exclaimed. "He is alive. Deepti and I both talked to him."

"My dear Sir, that can't be. Francis and his wife were both killed after their car crashed at the very spot your car crashed. Sir, I know this for a fact; I was his assistant and in the crew that brought their bodies in."

Arun was stunned and sat in silence.

"Inspector," came Deepti's voice from the other room.

"Francis had a young daughter named Mary, didn't he?"

"Why yes, Ma'am, how did you know that?"

"Francis told me so himself, Inspector."

• • •

The cemetery near the Holy family's Church was well-maintained, and there was dew on the grass. The air was fresh, and, unlike the unloved graves further away, here Francis Pinto's and his wife's graves were covered in bright blooms.

Mary tried to recollect when she attended the funeral mass for her deceased parents. Despite the greenery, she didn't know what season it was. After all, it was thirty years ago to the day when the accident befell them. But she could recall the details of that day better than any other. Friends and relatives had gathered to pay last respects to the kind and noble police officer and his wife and give comfort to his only daughter. Now orphaned.

Mary placed the wreath on her parent's graves. She stood there for a few minutes and uttered a silent prayer under her breath.

"I love you, Dad and Mom. See you in Heaven."

The End

What's in the Name?

The village was a small settlement usually found in India's rural setting. It was larger than a "hamlet" but smaller than a town and had over five thousand inhabitants. Community sentiment was predominant. They shared their happiness and sorrow and were bound by age-old traditional practices.

On the positive side, the village was free from the hustle and bustle of city life and was peaceful, calm, quiet and full of greenery where one could breathe fresh air.

But on the negative side, the village was not only a hub of black magic and witchcraft but was also supposedly cursed. It was still a backward district in a remote place in South India, but the villagers were not averse to century-old rituals associated with black magic.

One new moon day, in the pitch dark of the night, the dogs in the village started howling, and other domestic animals joined the chorus. Some villagers gathered enough courage to tour the area and heard strange noises emanating from an abandoned house on the outskirts of the village. They refused to go near the dilapidated house and beat a hasty retreat.

The village head held meetings with the elders in the days that followed. Each narrated his version about the strange happenings in the village. They gathered a few trusted villagers and visited the abandoned house accompanied by a few younger men armed with crowbars and sickles to face the situation head-on.

The women followed them for half the distance and watched the villagers halt in front of the house. They intuitively knew that some wicked witchcraft practitioner had arrived and taken siege of the house and let some evil spirits guard him. They thought that this was a better option than facing the wrath of the women at home for doing nothing.

As they neared the abandoned house, the villagers noticed that the windows and the doors of the house were open to let in the light and air. The reflective light of day brought a million warm hues of brown, each as magical as the others, to the house's tiled roof. They were taken aback by the sudden transformation of the abandoned house.

The village head went near the steps of the house while others remained a few feet away.

"Is there anyone at home?" he called out loud. There was no answer. He moved forward, climbed the stone steps leading to the entrance, and called out again.

The man who dashed out almost looked like a wizard, but not quite. The witchcraft practitioners usually had long braided unkempt hair and wore loose black clothes; they smeared their faces with ashes, traditionally collected from the cremation grounds.

But, to their utter surprise, the villagers noticed that this man was dressed in 'modern clothes'. He wore scrubby jeans and a T-shirt. His hair was spiked like some boy band member.

But something about his eyes looked scary. Like inside that persona was a little devil. Then there was the device on his wrist; he hadn't meant for it to be seen. Inside the house, some punk indie music blared from a tape recorder in the background. With a single sweep, he peered at the peasants, his dark eyes settling on nothing and his face expressionless.

He was never like what they had imagined. They were flabbergasted. The village head hesitatingly stepped forward. "Who are you, Sir? Why have you come to our village and occupied this house? What is it you want from us?" The village head stammered and stuttered incoherently.

The man stared at him with a distasteful look on his face and stepped forward. He raised his voice so that those standing a few yards away could hear him.

"I'm a wizard. I am a modern-day practitioner of witchcraft. I am not like the naked fakirs you have seen doing mumbo-jumbo rituals. I am the wand and all the magic ingredients. I invent the spells; add magic words in the perfect combinations. I am a good wizard; a magician who is a good person has the power to conduct blessings to creation."

"But we do not want a practitioner of witchcraft amidst us. Please leave us alone and go to a distant place. The women and children are scared." The village head found some strength in his voice. He didn't want to look weak in front of the villagers.

"You don't seem to understand the importance of my presence in this village. Don't you know this village is cursed?"

A murmur went through the crowd, and the wizard raised his hand, signalling the villagers to be quiet.

"I am a good wizard working with and for the positive universal force. I have come here to help you. The days of the magicians of the dark art helped by the negative force are over."

"We don't know you and don't trust you. We don't understand what you are saying. And please remember, there are the good magicians too, --- who will share their abilities and teach us how it works. So please leave this village by sundown; otherwise, face our fury."

The village head was showing off his aggressive side. He then turned his back and walked swiftly towards the village, and the small crowd watching the drama silently followed him.

The wizard stood staring at the villagers until they were out of sight. He slowly turned back and went inside his secret chamber. He took a small package from a corner -- mumbled some incomprehensible words.

The wizard's altar was a raised structure or place used for worship or prayer, upon which he placed several symbolic and functional items. There was incense, candles, crystal. There were human bones and a skull.

When you cuss, appeal to negativity or ask for revenge, and genuinely mean for cruel things to happen to others, the demon spirits will hear that you because your tone is the dial tone of their demonic phones And once you utter these words with real intent, it is a spell, a prayer to the devil, and they answer it. And this is what the wizard did, kneeling in front of the alter, uttering guttural prayers and swaying vigorously.

A greenish hue began to glow from within the package, seeping through the cracks. Then a flame and a cloud of white smoke puffed up from the box and faded into the air.

The poor villagers had no clue what awaited their fate.

• • •

Therein lies the crux of this pernicious practice of witchcraft – it supposedly has the potential to do good or bad, depending on the practitioner's intentions. Whether it worked or not – its practitioner claimed he could guarantee results – the practice nonetheless had a hold on many people living there.

The house fire took all it could, yet the stone walls remained firm. Flames rose into the night as if they challenged the heavens.

The burnt-down house looked skeletal in the new light of the day as if an artist sketched it in charcoal. Outside, the village head and his family stood shell shocked. They had no clue how this could have happened.

The villagers came in droves and put out the fire. Soon, they all gathered around the village head and started whispering in hushed tones. Only a demon could have targeted the village head and caused this havoc. They decided to confront the wizard.

• • •

"I can destroy the demon that burnt down your home. You are lucky to be alive." The wizard roared in his deep and gruff voice after hearing the woes of the village head. "I warned you to be careful, but you wouldn't care."

"I am a conduit for the divine spirit, the magic given to me by the creator of the universe," he thundered. "By obeying my orders, you will remain pure of heart. And you will prosper and lead a peaceful life. Thus good witchcraft and miracles are the same things. Submit yourself to my orders. Come to me if you have problems with anyone, and I shall fix the problem in your favour."

The villagers hung their heads and said aloud 'yes' in unison.

"Visit me tomorrow morning at sunrise and bring freshly prepared food, liquor, clothing and some silver and gold coins. I'll show you the how to live peacefully," the wizard's voice took a softer condescending tone.

The crowd dispersed. No one in the village knew his name, where he came from and what was happening in the house he lived. They called him Mayappa in a hushed tone. 'Maya' means 'illusion' and 'Appa' means 'father'.

"Hand over to me any material used by the person who is inimical towards you – such as hair or a piece of cloth. I'll then perform certain rituals, praying to demons and devils to teach him a lesson."

A black rooster was usually sacrificed for every ritual, but the wizard was offered a dead prepubescent girl for significant tasks to appease the demons.

The wizard demanded a continuous supply of food, liquor, gold and silver coins in return for the favour.

"If you fail to fulfil your promise, the spell will backfire on you," the wizard used to warn the man who wanted to teach his enemy a lesson.

Many villagers made a beeline to the wizard Mayappa's house and introduced themselves to him, showing their friendly and unsuspecting side. They would report to Mayappa with names of their enemies, a piece of cloth they wore, and some hair strands.

Mayappa would smile and say how happy he was to live in the village and ensure their happiness for a bright future. And then he would retire to his room at the back of his house. Inside the mysterious room, he would carefully tag them and store them orderly. He had an old dog-eared register to enter their names in black ink.

The villagers had no idea of the power they were giving the wizard. Names carried the essence of a thing, and Mayappa's magic acted through them, tapping into hearts, minds, and bodies. Mayappa thought that he could put half the village under his thrall if he collected enough names and personal effects. He gloated that soon he would bring the entire village under his thrall and rule over them.

The name collection turned out to be a noose around the villager's neck. It could backfire any day. Any time. The wizard got by on dribbles of his power. He played the part of the old healer, the minor magician. He peddled tinctures, told the villagers to call him their local God, and ordered every house in the village to register its family members with him.

The villagers made a beeline to his house. Mayappa would smile and say how charmed he was to meet them with each new name. And then he would retire to his secret room and open a tattered book to record the new name.

The villagers strongly believed that the wizard Mayappa could drive demons out of houses and trees, even though they hardly knew him. They were ignorant that some people had called his bluff in the next village and almost hanged him from a tree. The cunning Mayappa had fled under a gibbous moon with nothing but some strange items of rituals and some ancient-looking dog-eared books. Two guards had paid the price for listening to his mesmerizing talks.

• • •

Months passed. Mayappa's influence grew. The villagers kept greeting him respectfully from a distance, not crossing his path. They met all his daily needs for a comfortable living. There was an unending supply of food, liquor, clothes, fruits and other items for his daily needs.

Mayappa continued to collect the details of the villagers. It had become less of a precaution and more of a habit. In the middle of the night, after performing some rituals, he would open the register and look at how spidery writing filled the page, the way the alphabet linked together to form hundreds of different people. Each name carried stories. He knew that the villagers would sneak in when no one was looking and give him details of the person they wanted out of their way.

Mayappa thought everything was in his favour and the entire village was under his control – until, one day, a newcomer arrived.

• • •

The stranger came with hollowed cheeks and baggy torn cloths. He had dirt on his face, and braided hair hung from all sides of his face. He stood at the entrance of the house and started begging for food.

Upset for being disturbed from his afternoon siesta, Mayappa called him inside. The young man followed him quietly. Mayappa served the man rice gruel, bread and cooked vegetable and called it magic.

There was a cracked smile on the younger man's face – wry and small, but present, all the same.

Mayappa smiled back. "What's your name, young man? Would you like to work for me? I'll take care good care of you?"

The young man hesitated. "What's your name? What kind of job will you give me?"

This unexpected response from the young man gave the elder wizard, Mayappa, a pause. 'Who is this man asking for my name? He looks dangerous'. His eyes bore into the young man's body for the first time.

He eyed the hunting knife strapped to the man's belt, the splotch of skin on his arm that looked suspiciously like a burn mark, and the mysterious way the young man watched him. He thought this mystery man was a person who knew the value of a name. He may be someone who could threaten his place in the village.

While talking to him sweetly, he surreptitiously looked at the axe he had kept near the door. One of those mad moments would never have taken place had Mayappa paused to reason. Like the wind, the young man ran to the door where the axe was kept, grabbed the axe and swung before Mayappa could realize what was happening. Mayappa's head fell in slow motion and rolled away. His eyes stared at the young man, and his lips moved. And the darkness flooded his eyes.

After a few minutes, the young man picked up the blood-stained head and stepped outside. He saw a few villagers gathered a few feet away from the hose and staring at him in utter disbelief and shock. He then lifted the head of Mayappa and let out a war cry.

"You are now out of the wretched demon's spell. Go home now."

The villagers cheered as he went inside the house and bolted the wooden doors firmly from inside.

The following day, the sun's golden rays brightened the clouds and the village's rice fields. The first glimmering rays of sunlight shone through tall trees.

The young man looked at an older man sitting in front of him. He had a silver plate full of food and silver coins and eagerly looked at the young man. "This is all I have. Would you please help me? I am being troubled by a man..."

Gently, the young man set down his mug of tea and took the dog-eared register next to him. He took a black coloured pen and looked intently at the man for a few seconds. And asked:

"What's his name?"

The End

Banana Seller

At daybreak, Delhi has a Zen-like tranquilly. The city is the most accommodating before the heat raises temperatures and tempers. Whether it is flowers like roses, sunflowers or gerberas, or plants such as croton or even fruits like banana, guava or grape, everything is available at sunrise. Many hawkers open at about six in the morning and get a steady stream of early morning visitors.

Morning arrived as a mother's gentle hand, inviting night's dreams to enter the day. The sun shone brightly on the city.

It was time for offices to open, and office-goers started crowding towards the municipal office. It was the century-old heritage building full of emotions, stories of people who worked their entire life there.

My office was in a swank building bang opposite this building, and I had a fine view of the goings-on surrounding the building. I worked as an accounts executive in an auditing firm.

I noticed a woman standing alone in front of the municipal council building like a stone statue one fine day. She was an older woman, small built, but with a face having an aura of mystery. She carried a cane basket containing ripe bananas on her head. She had placed it on a twisted piece of cloth set on her head for grip; else, it would fall. She would lower the basket holding it with her hands as if for others to see the bananas. But after a few minutes, she would raise the basket again. Then she would make some strange hand gestures.

Sitting on a nearby compound wall, a monkey gibbered but wouldn't go near her. People passed by her as if they hadn't seen her. I thought she was soliciting buyers, but I was wrong because I didn't see anyone approaching her. After raising and lowering the banana basket several times, she left casually.

I thought she was too old to do the selling aggressively and did not belong to this age. I saw her lips moving as if she was talking to herself. For many days after that, every time I saw the woman, she was in the same place at the same time. She kept repeating her actions, and I kept wondering about the meaning of her actions.

Gradually, I started losing curiosity about her. One fine day, the woman disappeared. Occasionally in my free time, I used to think, '*Ah, where did that old banana seller go?*' There was no sign of her. I continued carrying out my boring accountant's work, and the old banana seller gradually faded from my memory.

Until a rainy day.

The weather was gloomy and terrible that day and the clouds in the leaden sky were low as if they were about to collapse at any time.

The old lady suddenly appeared with the basket on her head and was standing at the same place. I was busy tallying my company's accounts on my computer, and I saw her when I raised my head and stretched to relax my back.

And she turned her head towards me. I smiled and waved as if I saw a long-lost aunt and went back to my work feeling relieved, thinking she was safe. But as soon as I raised my head, I saw the basket on the ground, and the old lady was not to be seen.

'*Could it be that she has gone to meet someone?*' I thought, but she didn't show up for quite some time.

Instead, a monkey stood near the basket and screamed miserably, sounding like a baby crying. A primal scream was calling out for help. My hair stood upright by the sound. I just wanted to see the monkey. But the basket and the monkey were gone in the blink of an eye.

Later, unable to rein in my curiosity, I wandered the area searching for the older woman and found a woman smoking a cheap rolled cigarette, sheltered under a banyan tree staring at me. Hesitatingly, I approached her and enquired about the banana seller.

She gestured to come near her and whispered, "She is a witch. She practices black magic. Be careful."

I was taken aback and stepped back a few feet away from her. She laughed.

"Many years ago, as a young woman, she worked in the municipal office in a low-paid job and during her free time, she sold bananas outside the office premises. She was having an affair with a colleague who had promised to marry her. She waited outside the building for her companion the entire day and night on the designated day, but he never showed up."

"I understand she went wild with blind fury. People were gossiping that she had murdered him. Nothing was proven. She continued to work for the municipal office till the time she retired. Years didn't cool down her temper, and she started hating men who cheated on their partners."

The woman paused as if to recollect some unsavoury past events and continued. "She would find out about such cheating men, then go to their residences with the basket of bananas and a monkey and cast some spell on the man living there. Soon the curse would take effect, and the person would meet with an unnatural death. Her curse ensured that his soul would enter the monkey."

Unable to swallow the weird story, I asked her mockingly, "Where did those people who became monkeys go?"

"I don't know. But the witch had lots of monkeys in her custody keeping a watch on her. The municipal authorities would never catch them."

"What about families of the affected people? Did they not take any action against the witch?"

"No. The people were too scared to even talk about It?"

"I think it is very cruel of the woman to do that. I would hand over the witch to the police and see to it she was locked up for life."

"Why do you say that?" the woman was visibly upset.

"After becoming a monkey, the man will live forever happily eating and drinking every day. No worldly responsibilities. Being human is too boring and taxing."

I kept silent for a while, and to avoid an unpleasant confrontation, I said in a conciliatory tone, "Maybe you have a point there. This witch had a bad temper, but she was not a vicious person."

"Of course not. On the contrary, she was a very kind person."

To my surprise, the woman suddenly got up and left. She had a weird dancing gait; her footsteps were light, like a performing monkey in a roadshow.

Then I saw the basket of bananas behind the tree and a monkey guarding it. It started doing some noisy tantrums. I looked back.

The woman had disappeared.

Hearing some unusual noise, I looked up, and my heart skipped a beat. I saw many monkeys staring down at me from the banyan tree.

I broke out in a cold sweat and beat a hasty retreat.

The End

Close Encounter

Sunset is an incredible sight to watch from a beach in Mumbai. The beautiful mixing of colours in the evening sky provides a fabulous view. The sunset came in its boldest blaze as if God sprayed *Holi* colours upon the evening sky.

Inspector Shinde was on his routine patrol, keeping a close watch on the locals and the tourists.

It was getting late, and Shinde felt that the air was taking on the chill. He was getting ready to return to his office and hand over charge to his night-shift colleague. As he was about to start the petrol car, the police radio sprang to life.

"Hello, I'm calling from the police commissioner's office. Am I speaking with Inspector Shinde?"

The caller spoke authoritatively, and his orders were crisp and clear. He asked Shinde to immediately inspect an abandoned building in a slum area of the National Park area and report his findings by the following day.

"There appears to be some problem brewing in that locality. Please take note that it is a cabinet minister's constituency. Do a thorough job. No bungling." Before he could respond, the phone at the other end went dead.

Shinde took nearly an hour to reach the slum that had sprouted on the National Park's dark side. The dwellings were unfit for human habitation because of dilapidation, overcrowding and unhygienic conditions.

Shinde was aware that the crumbling abandoned building near the slum gave many gangsters and anti-social elements safe shelter. The spooky house breathed deep and long whispers in the embrace of deep shadows. In the brindled light of dusk, the creepy house was ready to play.

Shinde slowed down as he pulled the car over to the kerb near the abandoned building. A bunch of older people standing near the building approached him.

"How are you, people? Who has given a complaint to the Police HQ? What's the problem?" Shinde's voice betrayed his annoyance.

An older adult who looked like the chief of that area came forward. "Annoyed and scared. That's how we are feeling! The kids are afraid, and the elderly are unable to sleep. Every night for the past few days, much noise, howling comes from that building. Sometime back, some anti-social men had occupied that building."

"What noise?" Shinde queried. "Everything is quiet here. I don't hear a thing that can be called disturbing!"

"We were hoping you could find out what is causing all those disturbing noises and put a stop to it. We want you to find out what is causing all those disturbing noises and put a stop to it. We are tired of complaining every day. But no authority seems to care. We may be living in slums, but we are honest citizens. We demand peace at night!"

"Very well, I'll check it out," Shinde said, trying to cover his yawn.

A half-suppressed murmur went through the crowd, and they turned and stormed back into their dwellings.

Shinde sighed and called his superior, "Sir, I have reached the slum. I see the abandoned building close to the slum. It looks very shady and is the root cause of the unrest here. I might as well check it out now that I'm here."

He took out his flashlight and gestured the guys' leader to lead the way. He followed him to the building, and they entered the front door. Shinde scanned the place with his sharp eyes, took out his cell phone and took a couple of shots.

He found the place deserted. There was no one there, and the place resembled a devil's haunt. It looked like a war-torn area. Shinde carefully avoided stepping on broken glass and checked around, including upstairs, downstairs and the basement. There was simply nothing there.

"See anything?" the old man asked him.

Shinde laughed aloud, and the echo of little voices inspired several snickers from around them.

"Can't you guys check for yourselves? You seem to be a bunch of cowards."

Suddenly, a strange sound came to them, and they looked at each other.

"What was that?" the old man asked in a shivering voice.

Shinde shrugged. "I don't know. I think it was an echo of my laugh."

They rushed back to the door and quickly got outside. Shinde breathed a sigh of relief and made his way to the car. As he climbed in, a woman came running from one dwelling.

"What was making all the horrible noises? Did you find out?" she demanded.

"No," Shinde told her. "We checked the place in, and out and there is nothing there."

Shinde sighed and continued to address the man. "It happens all the time when you guys get drunk. You'll hear strange noises in your head. Possibly, you heard some noises coming from your slum in your neighbourhood. I have checked, and I am sure that there is no noise, or no sound at all, coming from that building."

The woman turned and walked back into her shanty without uttering another word. Shinde headed back home.

• • •

It was close to midnight as Shinde headed home. He received another call from dispatch. The voice at the other end barked, "We have received serious complaints from the slum dwellers that you abandoned the search midway. Everyone seems to be having a cell phone. Your flippant behaviour is unacceptable."

The man at the other end ordered Inspector Shinde to head back to the dilapidated building. "Make sure you do a thorough search. Take those people into confidence and pacify them. The minister is closely following the case."

Shinde swore under his breath and turned around towards the foul place. As he approached the area, a couple of women came storming down from the road. "It's happening again!" they screamed. "It just stopped as you pulled up!"

Shinde climbed out of the car, and as he looked over at the house, he saw a figure entering through the front door!

"Hey, who's that?" he demanded.

The leader of the slum shook his head, as well, but said, "I don't know who he is. I have no idea, but I've seen him come and go through the front door a few times, always at night."

Suddenly there was a massive blast of noise coming from the building!

"What the hell...." Shinde was shocked and shouted as the lady in the group gestured to him, "I told you many times. You wouldn't care to listen."

Shinde reached into the car for a flashlight. He motioned to a couple of guys to follow him. Together they made their way to the derelict home. As they neared the building, lights suddenly appeared in every window, and Shinde was agitated. "What the hell is going on?" he shouted.

The small crowd was getting scared. As they reached the front steps, everything died. No lights, no noise, nothing. They looked at each other apprehensively and went in.

The same scene as when they entered the first time was visible – no one, nothing else, nothing but deep darkness. There was a slight difference, however. Shinde felt as if there was a presence as if there was someone there. He looked firmly about, but there was simply no one present. He turned to the guys, "I'll check the upstairs; you look around here."

Shinde took out his flashlight and shone it everywhere he could. Suddenly a man was standing before him!

"Looking for something?" he asked him softly.

Shinde jumped up a mile in shock. "Who are you?" he demanded.

"No offence, Sir, but I didn't permit you to enter my house."

"I ask again. Who in the hell are you?" Shinde put on his brave front.

"I'mnobody, really," answered the man calmly. "I exist here. Whom are you looking for?"

"If you're the one making that frightful racket all night long, then you're my guy."

"I do get a bit boisterous and brash at times."

"You are not a drug addict. And you wouldn't happen to have any dope in your place would you?"

"Of course not!"

"Then you wouldn't mind if I take a look, would you?"

"Ummmm. **Yes, Sir, I do mind. I respect my privacy.**"

"Well, mister, you're in much trouble! **I do not need your consent to a search.**"

"May I go now, please? I want to remain silent, and I want my lawyer."

"Who in the hell are you?"

"I told you I'm nobody. I'm not in hell. Not yet."

"Really? You have to be somebody!"

"Oh, I was, at one time. I am no longer. Can I show you around?"

"What? Sure!"

The man took Shinde to what looked like a bedroom.

"Here it is."

"Here what is?"

"The somebody you're looking for."

Inspector Shinde shone the torch around and was in for a rude shock. He noticed there was a dead body lying on the broken cot. He had been dead over a long time, judging by the level of decomposition. The bed was coloured with what looked like dried blood.

"I told you."

"OMG! You are in deep trouble now. Who is this?"

"You mean who *was* this," the man replied with studied composure.

"All right, all right, who was this?"

"Just somebody who used to live here. Now he's dead here."

"Are you some comedian?" Shinde was getting irritated.

"You guessed it right. I worked in a few Bollywood movies till I fell into bad company."

"What do you mean ... Er...bad company? Drug dealers?"

"Yup. Unfortunately, I fell out of favour with them in one of the deals, and they bumped me off."

"What is going on here?" Shinde repeated himself nervously and looked at his watch. "Look. I've no time for small talks. I am going to call the police station for backup."

"Well, I have no further information to give you. I better enter my body again, if you don't mind."

The man vanished.

Shinde looked around wildly. "Hey, where did you go?"

Then he heard someone groaning and slowly turned around. The dead body was there, climbing to its feet.

"Hey, how about that? I'm somebody again! Great, isn't it? A some-body from no-body," it said and started to laugh.

It was the most dreadful sound Shinde had ever heard, and he raced for the stairs! He practically flew down in panic and ran out the front door!

The crowd had disappeared. Shinde got into car and looked back at the building. The body closed on him, mutilated and covered with dried blood.

"Wait, don't run," it called. "Come back. Don't you want to arrest somebody?" And it made the fearful sound again.

Shinde never did go back. He begged the HQ to transfer to another city the following day, where the dead remained dead.

The End

The Pink Dress

The dress slid upon her skin as soft petals, its hue the many pinks of a rose garden. In the hug of the dress, her spirit soared, buoyed by the carefree breeze.

She was in a new relationship with Arun, and she felt an emotional connection with him on a deeper soul level. This new relationship was a new day, a fresh start, a clean slate.

Arun gave his girlfriend Anna an appreciative once-over. A common friend had introduced them. They had kept their relationship a secret because he believed it would put too much strain on them.

The following weekend Arun had given her a present, an elegant looking dress made in France. She was excited. She thought he was the most thoughtful person she had met.

"Let's keep this between us until the time is right," he said.

The next day Anna wore her new dress and walked into the city.

It wasn't until many folks left and the street became empty that she noticed strange-looking graffiti. As she watched it, there was movement. She felt that the graffiti moved.

She then saw a black figure, and it was vaguely humanoid. It looked like black scribbles, but the scribbles moved like electricity arcing. As it came into focus, Anna could see the form of a woman with bloody ragged lines across her neck and pale soulless eyes.

Anna's heart felt like a terrified bird, slamming inside her chest. She couldn't catch her breath. She started to run.

She couldn't run wearing her flowing dress. '*Why is it that the only thing that made me feel free again now makes me feel trapped?*' Anna muttered to herself.

It was getting dark, and the approaching night was teasing the sky into twilight. Anna walked as fast as she could. By the time she got home, night had fallen and enveloped the city in a blanket of darkness. She scurried down the path towards her house. The metal of the doorknob was cool against her palm, and she twisted it with ease, entering the dark living room. Suddenly her eyes became glassy and vacant.

Anna distinctly remembered when she saw the strange woman's figure. It was the graffiti. She didn't move, didn't scream, did nothing. She was just frozen.

A hand on her shoulder pulled her out of her thoughts.

"Hello Darling, you all right?" the woman said. There was cold concern in the woman's voice, and she knelt in front of her.

"Who are you?" an agonized expression came over Anna's face. Her throat hurt, and it came out as a hoarse whisper.

"We need to talk about Arun," the woman replied sternly, unsmiling.

"Is Arun all right? I will call him right now," pleaded Anna.

"He can't answer you silly; he's sleeping, deep sleep," the woman sniggered.

"What the hell are you talking about? I will kill you if you've hurt him," Anna suddenly lunged at her and fell.

The woman let out an obnoxious laugh. "Threats are not nice. Why did you have to make me miserable? I was happy, properly happy in love. Arun loved me, but you entered his life and ruined it," the woman's voice took on a dejected tone.

"What are you talking about? Are you mental?"

"Arun was my lover," the woman sneered, her voice full of spite and threat.

"What have you done to him?" Anna was panicking now, and her voice showed it.

"Shut up. This isn't about Arun anymore. It's about me, and you have ruined my whole life."

The woman had a deranged look on her face.

"I'm sorry for whatever happened between Arun and me. If you let me go, I will make it right. I promise."

"Thanks, Anna. Too late for that now. I know he was having an affair with you on the sly. I was already entwined in his life. The pink dress you are wearing belonged to me."

Anna slumped, anger and fight replaced entirely by fear and helplessness.

The woman ranted, "I loved him; he loved me. But you entered the picture and stole him from me. I ended my life out of sheer frustration. And I had no choice but to take him with me. Now we are going to be together forever. I know you understand."

"No, I don't understand. Who are you?" Anna didn't get any further.

Her voice was taken away by the blade that was now going through her throat. Her eyes widened as she looked at the woman's figure still smiling at her.

Anna tried to move. She tried to shout. But her energy was draining fast.

She needed to lie down. She needed to close her eyes. She needed to let the darkness set in.

The woman looked down at the corpse. The knife stuck out of her throat. Blood pooled on the floor. She reached down and removed the dress.

"Arun told me only I looked best in this pink dress."

She blew a kiss at the corpse and then floated out of the house.

The End

Hills Have Eyes

In the middle of January 2000, the fear of Y2K had passed. No plane was falling from the sky, and all electronic networks worked well. The early morning flight from Mumbai to Bhubaneswar took off on time. The captain came on and gave a little speech about the flight. The flight attendants got busy with their routine.

Mahesh Agrawal groaned loudly. The flight's expected duration was two hours and fifteen minutes. The take-off was a bumpy roller coaster ride. Agrawal braced himself on the seat in front. Once in the air, things felt smooth. He took out a small map of a mine from his briefcase and started studying it. He was excited at the prospects of acquiring an iron ore mine near a village called Kirimuri in the resource-rich state of Odisha. The attractive sale proposal had landed on his lap from a chance interaction with a local contact.

Agrawal didn't want the opportunity to slip through his fingers. The Chinese were starving for high-grade ore from India and were prepared to pay twice the local rates. Agrawal studied the market and travelled to Hong Kong to tie up with buyers as a shrewd businessman. He decided that this was a golden opportunity to make a 'quick buck' and establish his name as an industrialist.

Agrawal was tired of being a broker selling licences; the commissions were shrinking in that business. He floated a company, 'Agrawal Mining Enterprises', to carry out mining activities and export the iron ore to China without wasting time.

As the aircraft approached the landing, Agrawal let out a yawn to ease the pressure on his eardrums. The landing was pretty gentle and less harsh than a speed bump. As soon as the plane landed, Agrawal quickly got off the aircraft. He was in haste to leave the airport, as the mine was quite far from the city. He was relieved to find Gopal Mohanty, his contact in Bhubaneswar, waiting for him with a placard in hand.

"Good Morning, Agrawal Sir," Mohanty greeted him cheerfully, taking Agarwal's luggage. "Welcome to Odisha."

"Good to see you, Mohanty," Agrawal replied enthusiastically. "I hope you have made all the arrangements for my visit to the mines."

"Not to worry, Sir. I have brought a large, sturdy vehicle, and we can head to the mines straightaway. To save time, I have also brought some refreshments for the journey."

Agrawal was pleased, and they walked silently towards the car parking.

"Let me give you the background of this mine, Sir," Manoj Das, a retired mining officer, said after clearing his throat. Agarwal had hired him as a technical consultant for Agrawal Mining Enterprises. He began filling him in with all technical details and prospects of the mining industry, which of course, was seen as rosy as ever. He was accompanying Agrawal to the mines. They had left the city and were on their way to the mines.

"According to the government records, the rights to mining iron ore were given to one Mr Jagannath Mohapatra many years ago. This mine is spread over 100 hectares and is estimated to have 25 million tonnes of iron ore." Manoj Das paused for effect and to catch his breath. Agrawal raised his eyebrows in astonishment. He had never heard of such a rich mine being offered for outright sale. And that too at half the price.

• • •

The road to Kirimuri village, where the mine was situated, looked like it was carved out of hillocks and forests. Due to the spectacular beauty of its surroundings, the road was frequented despite its fearsome reputation for craters, rock falls, landslides, reckless drivers, herds of animals, precipitous cliffs. It took them a little over six hours to get to the mines.

They passed through the sparsely populated village of Kirimuri and reached the mine. Agrawal was the first to get out of the van and walk towards the mine, a mile away. There was no approach road. There was only plain uneven land with boulders of various sizes stretching from the rough road to the mine head. It was then that he felt something – he felt the small hillocks looking at him through many eyes.

He turned towards Manoj Das, who animatedly talked to the small group of locals who had come to meet them. It appeared they were in a serious argument with Das.

"Das, how much ore has already been mined from this site? Any idea? I don't see many excavations done here."

"Yes. It's true, Sir," Das nodded his head. He motioned the villagers to keep a distance." The owner was very keen to develop this village, and the mine was an ideal project for him to employ the locals. But things didn't work out as he wished..." his voice trailed off.

"What was the reason?" Agrawal queried. "Had he continued, he could have minted money and become a trendy man as well."

"Unfortunately, he turned out to be a very superstitious and a weak-hearted guy," Das said. "Once he started mining, domestic problems cropped up for him. First, he fell sick and had to be hospitalized." Das paused to take a deep breath before he continued. "Later, his family moved out and shifted to the city. He was left alone to fend for himself, but he didn't lose heart and continued mining."

"But the mine had different plans for him. On the third day, it swallowed three miners. There was no trace of them at the end of the day. The villagers were agitated. They felt that some evil force was at play and were scared for their lives. They said they heard some screams emanating from the mines at night."

"No amount of inducements would make them change their mind. But Mohapatra didn't lose his courage and heart. He brought a strong workforce from a neighbouring village and some earthmoving machinery to continue the mining work."

"But after two days of work, three more workmen went missing in the mines, and two of his earthmoving machines toppled from the top as if some colossal hand had pushed them down. The Mining Safety Department pounced on the place and sealed the mine. Mohapatra went into liquidation, spending a considerable amount buying and developing this mine. He had borrowed heavily from banks and friends. He had no choice but to sell the mine and clear his loan and avoid going to jail."

Agrawal listened to him silently without interrupting. He walked towards the mine and kept staring at it for some time. It was a hot afternoon and Agrawal was sweating profusely. He wiped his face with his handkerchief and returned to sit in the comfort of his car.

"Can you explain to me what those things are that look like eyes?" he asked Das.

Das laughed. "Those are the preliminary excavations to take out samples of the iron ore. They have to be done at various places as per the rules." Das continued as though he was taking a class. "You see, Sir, the ore body generally forms the tops of the ridges and hillocks. That is what you see here. It is called an open pit or open cast mining."

Agrawal shrugged and nodded his head in agreement. "Let's go to the guest house," he said after a minute. "I have come from Mumbai not to get frightened by some weird story. Let's meet the owner, Mohapatra, tomorrow and close the deal. I am sure we can find a way to resolve this issue."

The guest house was in the corner of the village. It was sparsely furnished but clean. It had a beautiful view of the mountains, and in the evening, there was a sunset that gave a fantastic golden hue to the sky. There was no further talk about the mines, and they all took a well-deserved rest.

• • •

"Yes. It is true what Manoj Das has told you about the unusual happenings in the mine," Jagannath Mohapatra drawled. He had invited Agrawal for lunch at his home the next day and served him a sumptuous local meal. "As a mining engineer, he had created mining surveys for developers in the region. He was thorough in his work. Based on his technical work, I bought the mine for a 99-year lease. It was my bad luck that wouldn't let me progress with the mining."

He paused for a few seconds before continuing, "Maybe the mine will bring you better luck." Agrawal just nodded his head smiled. After the meeting, Agrawal excused himself and assured Mohapatra that he was still interested in the mines. He would revert to him next after talking to his partner.

• • •

"When you have that in the back of your mind, it stimulates something," Agrawal was talking to his partner back home as soon as he returned to his room. "Of course, my people here thought all these unusual happenings were due to some mischief of wicked spirits. The mines all around it have not reported any such happening. I think it is a farce to prevent us from acquiring the mine."

"The mines did not gobble up those workers. They must have just run away to different mines offering better pay. And the machines tumbled down because of loose soil and human negligence." His partner agreed and asked him to go ahead and close the deal.

He spent the next three days fixing a lawyer to draw up the Agreement of Sale of the mines. Agrawal and Mohapatra quickly signed and registered the sale papers upon completing the agreements. Agrawal paid the amount in full to Mohapatra and rewarded his men generously. They decided to gear up for the work with men and machinery and start work in ten days. Agrawal told them that he was leaving for Mumbai on some urgent assignment and would be back for the initial ground-breaking ceremony. He put Das in charge of the whole operation and asked them to report daily.

• • •

The mining work began within a short time, and the following days (and nights) were uneventful.

On a full moon day, the problem began to surface. The shrill tone of the cell phone next to his bed made Agrawal jump out of bed. He noted that the time was 5.30 a.m., and it was Mohanty. He seemed beside himself in panic.

"Agrawal Sir, you need to come over here immediately. Some severe problems have cropped up, and the work has stopped."

"Who is creating problems?" Agrawal questioned angrily.

"The mine, Sir!"

Agrawal let out a cuss word and told him he would try to catch the next available flight to Bhubaneswar, and he should meet him at the airport along with the mining expert Das. He quickly got ready and left for the airport.

• • •

"What is the problem, gentlemen? Why have you called me in such great haste?" Agrawal queried as they said down to have a cup of tea in a restaurant in the airport.

Mohanty was looking nervous, and Das was somewhat composed.

"Day before yesterday was the full moon day," he paused, not knowing how to break the story.

"So?" Agrawal interrupted and raised his eyebrows.

"It's not the first time you are seeing it, is it?" his voice dripping with sarcasm. "You have called me over from Mumbai to tell me this?"

"No, Sir!" Das was apologetic. "We are sorry to have disturbed you. Something terrible has happened in the village, and the villagers are angry and scared. They came in hordes and stopped the work. They beat up some workers we had hired from the neighbouring village in an altercation. The emotion was running high."

"Das, please don't beat around the bush," Agrawal looked at him sternly. "Please tell me what happened at the mines."

Das took a deep breath and started narrating the incident.

"Miners, like sailors and fishermen, believe in omens. But their beliefs and superstitions might not make sense to other people. According to the villagers of Kirimuri, the mine is infested with ghosts of some dead miners. They hear their cries in the night, and some passer-by told the villagers he saw three figures standing atop the hillock with torches in their hands. They had no faces. Villagers believed that dead miners continued to haunt the mine despite all kinds of efforts to drive them away. Glowing torches were reported to be seen near the mine at night. They heard the sound of cries. They said they felt a brooding presence of spirits that made strong men weak by the sheer impact of palpable fear. They feel that the spirits want to be left alone, and the mine should be left untouched."

Mohanty was sitting still as if someone had cast a spell on him and was staring at the floor. Das nudged him and asked him to continue, and started sipping water. Das sipped water from his glass and continued.

"Day before was a full moon night, and that night several women in the village were possessed by evil spirits. The 'possessed' women were taken to the local shrine to be exorcized. Villagers who brought their wives, daughters and relatives here felt the women's bodies had been taken over by souls of the dead and that exorcism was the only release for them. Interestingly, those who come here to be exorcized were women."

"Why only women?" Agrawal queried.

"That is because the villagers think they are emotionally weak and hence easy targets for the spirits," Mohanty butted in immediately, making Agrawal squirm in his chair.

"What a bunch of ignorant people!" he told himself, not displaying his irritation.

"Some women suffered temporary attacks, which means they are fine one minute and the next they start jumping, screaming, crying or even attacking people. The temple becomes chaotic just before dusk when ghosts attack more and more women." Mohanty was talking like an expert in paranormal activity.

Mohanty paused to control his nerves. "We had an unfortunate accident in our mines three days ago, and a miner lost his life when a boulder collapsed on him. We called in rescue. It was just after sunset, and seven people went to the iron ore hillock to bring back the body, but only five returned. The search for the missing guys is on. I confess it was just eerie up there in the hillock. The villagers want the mine to be shut down entirely and sealed, barring entry for anyone."

"Gentlemen," Agrawal raised his hand, motioning them to stop. "Enough of this crap! I've checked with knowledgeable people in the business, and there are some things you need to know about the mines. It is pretty standard, very typical actually, to hear strange sounds coming from forests and deserted hillsides. It is common to see lights that aren't supposed to be there and listen to voices that aren't there. There is moonshine over shiny boulders, which reflect light making them look like fire, and the animals howl in the night. There is nothing unusual about it."

"But Sir," Das interjected. "Villagers also say it is common to see lights, hear voices, and even see torches from time to time. Most men who work in the mine accept it and just go about their job. I have heard such stories throughout my long career, and I never feared it because other miners were always right there with me."

"You know there is safety in numbers. But this time, things have gone beyond my control, and the villagers are very upset and have panicked."

Agrawal sat in silence, deep in thought. The other two were looking at him expectantly.

"I have heard you. Now listen to me," Agrawal said in a calm voice. "Let's go meet with the village head and explain to him the ground realities. Let's convince him that we should make progress and not get carried away by some weird ghost stories. Let's assure him that we will hire only the local villagers for all the mining activities, and I will pay them well. A handsome compensation to him in his capacity should tilt the case in our favour."

Das and Mohanty meekly nodded. They hurriedly left for the mine. Things worked out well for Agrawal during the meeting with the village head, villagers and the head-priest at the local temple. They met them separately, distributed cash, liquor and sweets.

Agrawal was assured of their cooperation. The village head said in a stern voice, "Sir, you may start the work. But if anything happens to the villagers, we will seal the mines and won't allow anyone to come near it."

Agrawal gave him his benevolent smile. "Not to worry," he assured. "Everything is taken care of."

Nobody understood what he meant. Neither did he, for that matter. It was one of those jargons he had picked up from his politician friends!

"Now let's visit the mine," urged Agrawal to Das and Mohanty. "Start mobilizing people and machinery. I will have to inspect the mine myself. Otherwise, there is no way to find out the real story behind this drama."

Das and Mohanty were a bit reluctant. "Sir, it will soon be dark, and I suggest we carry out the inspection first thing tomorrow morning."

"No way," said Agrawal in a firm tone. "Let it get dark. I would like to see the spirits and shake hands with them. They will be carrying torches and will show us the way to reach the top."

He was sarcastic and laughed at his joke. Das and Mohanty looked glum; they glanced at each other and shrugged.

• • •

Soon they reached the mine, accompanied by a few villagers. Agrawal quickly got out of the vehicle and started moving closer to the bottom of the hill. He cautiously checked the surface and kept an eye on the mountain. Das, Mohanty and six sturdy men followed him. All along the way, they cautioned him about the unevenness of the surface lest he should sprain his ankle or worse.

Agrawal slowed midway abruptly. He had a strange feeling that the pathway leading to the hill wasn't quite right. It was too perfect. He bent down and grabbed an iron ore rock nearest to him and held it close to his eyes. He picked up a few more for close examination. They were of the same size and had the same reddish colour. Agrawal instantly realized that the ore was of high quality. But unnatural, he thought, like a modern extraction machine had been sunk into the earth and expertly extracted the ore. This occurrence can't be natural, he thought. The day wasn't cold, but Agrawal shivered.

He dropped the rock. Suddenly the wind changed directions, rattling dead leaves all around him. Other than that, there was no sound. One of the villagers was coughing loudly. Das was panting, and everyone had stopped. He threw another rock far. But Agrawal didn't hear it land anywhere.

The smell of burning flesh came a few seconds later. Everyone stood still. And the smell of the earth that hits one's nostrils after a blast by dynamite filled the air.

Agarwal's eyes rolled back in his head as he swayed. He caught his balance but dropped to one knee. Such a lovely, beckoning scent, he told himself. He feared the worst and then crawled towards the hill, which was closer than he thought.

He felt the ground against his chest and realized that he had fallen flat on his stomach. His back arched. His legs twisted, toes pushing at the ground. Then he raised his head and came face to face with the hill staring at him. He grinned like a mad man and stared back, panting and was more content than he'd ever known. He thought he had found the perfect and pure mine, full of red iron ore to last for a couple of generations.

The men behind him were watching the strange sight in stupefied silence. Agarwal raised his hand and motioned them not to come near him. He got up and sat down and was looking at the hill mournfully. The flashlight fell from his hand and rolled away. He started crawling towards the edge of the ridge. The men ran towards him, then halted mid-stride and approached him cautiously. They gently picked him up, carried him to the vehicle and drove back as fast as possible.

• • •

Agrawal lay confined to his bed in the guest house for three days. Almost in delirium. The doctor from the city told Das that his life was not in danger and he should take complete rest for some time.

As he lay in bed, Agrawal lost sense of time, and with that, his memories started to fail him. Some days later, at an unknown time, his eyes flickered open as he sensed movement. "Mohanty? Das?" he called out feebly. "What happened? Why am I here? How did I get here? Why am I all alone?" But there was no one.

He felt there was something, however. His head was bandaged. He must have banged his head on the rock while going towards the hill. He tried to shout, mouth open, squeezed his eyes shut. He'd never felt such terror.

Agrawal thought he was dreaming. He felt the presence of a man in his room. Or at least a figure that had the outline of a man. Tall and thin. The figure bent down and looked deep into his eyes. He reached out and almost took his chin with his bony fingers, keeping his head still, paralyzing him without touching him.

Agrawal could smell burning flesh – it made him sick. It seemed familiar, but he couldn't recall.

"Don't go near the mine! Go back."

The figure pulled the head backwards, nodded and disappeared.

Agrawal felt he was running towards the mine. Falling. Crawling. He kept running with outstretched arms, but the distance did not decrease. He thought he was in a vacuum. It seemed like time had stopped. Soon, he saw his still figure surrounded by iron ore rocks, and his burial had begun.

• • •

"Do you know anything about this tall thin man, Sir? Can you recall anything?" Das was asking him. He had come into the room along with Mohanty.

Agrawal shook his head. He spoke quietly. "I thought I must have imagined it. But maybe it was a ghost." He kept quiet about the advice to not return to the hill.

"We're so lucky to have you back." He heard Mohanty's voice. He came close and smiled at him.

Agrawal tried to smile. "Keep it just between us for now about this tall thin man. Other people won't understand it. Don't tell the villagers or the village head. Just tell them I have a high fever and need rest. Okay?"

"Yes, Sir. We understand."

Agrawal winced in pain as he tried to prop himself up on the bed. He felt his body twitch, and he took a few deep breaths and brought his hand up to let his fingers examine his skull.

He rocked to and fro, mentally challenged his body parts, and felt happy that nothing was broken – only some bruises which would heal in a couple of days.

"Gentlemen," he said after clearing his throat. "What the villagers are talking about?"

"Nothing much, Sir. They want to know if you are going to continue the mining. They are worried for their jobs."

"That's good news," Agrawal smiled. "Give me three days to recover. And then let me make one more visit to the top of the hill."

They remained silent, and Mohanty spoke, "Sir, I suggest you go back to Mumbai and rest for a month. We will handle the work here. The villagers will cooperate. Not to worry." He looked at Das expectantly, who nodded in agreement.

"Look," Agrawal spoke sternly. "I'm not going back until I sort out this nuisance. I have spoken with my partner, and he will manage the affairs of the Mumbai office. All I need is your support now. Physical and mental."

The two remained silent. "Okay then. Let's make the trip to the top of the hill three days from now. I am sure I'll be fully recovered by then," Agrawal declared triumphantly.

"Let's do it on the full moon day. There will be enough moonlight to enable us to find out a way to the top."

Das and Mohanty looked at each other with widened eyes and left silently.

• • •

Three uneventful days passed, and Agrawal felt renewed vigour propelling him to go to the iron ore hills. His partner had called him to say that a couple of Chinese firms were already in touch with him and had agreed to sign the contract at his terms. He wished him a speedy recovery and good luck with the mining work.

Agrawal was up and ready, pacing his room much before his team arrived. There were six villagers with pickaxes and torches and sacks to carry samples. Agrawal insisted that he would climb up the hill first and that others should follow him. He advised Das and Mohanty to engage with the villagers and keep them in good humour.

They reached the foot of the hill in time. The entire area looked peaceful. Agrawal felt he had never observed its picturesque beauty before. He stood in silence and kept staring at the hill for a minute and then announced loudly,

"Let's go!"

The team was startled by the suddenness of his comment. He checked his powerful light torch, adjusted his cap, and slowly moved towards the hill.

Only the silent breeze that was combing through the treetops was audible. The men moved in pairs, in silence.

The hill was less visible, and the weak moon appeared behind a cloud. Agrawal looked up, stopped and looked back. His men were behind him, puffing their way up. He nodded his head in satisfaction and started his climb.

After a fifteen-minute climb, the moon had come out from behind the clouds and was shining brightly. That amplified their emotions and fears, as the hill looked even scarier as thick trunks of trees and awkwardly spread out branches looked like strange-limbed beasts.

Agrawal paused to catch his breath and looked around. When he looked up, he felt the hills had eyes and were staring at him.

'*Wait till I reach the top*', Agrawal muttered to himself. '*I am going to master you and blast you to pieces. The Chinese are waiting to take you home duly crushed.*'

He let himself a wry smile and continued. He looked around and found that the rocky mountain was steep and intimidating. There were huge rocks on either side of the track leading to the top of the hill.

'*Is this the place where I had fallen last time? That is where I got a head injury, right?*' he reassuringly spoke to himself. '*Once I get to the top and solve the mystery and remove the fears of the villagers, it would be easy to carry on with the mining work with full force.*'

Filled with his newfound determination, he started to climb the hill. He rose for a couple of minutes and sat down to rest for a minute. He noticed his people were quite far away and were slowly climbing up, swinging their flashlights wildly. He waved and shouted for the men to stop. *'This Mohanty guy should have brought younger and stronger men'*, he muttered to himself.

He started to climb again slowly but steadily until he reached a point right under the cliff. Climbing further was getting difficult. He let out a few curses and started searching for another route to reach the top. Suddenly, he found a stretch that led him directly to the top. To his amazement, Agrawal found that the top was as flat and as spacious as a football field filled with rocks and wild growth. It was obvious no one had reached the top so far.

He looked down and found his men pointing flashlights at him. The full moon was visible now in the clear sky. He surveyed the place and found a dense forest on the other side. He noticed that the path down the hill seemed to have disappeared.

Agrawal frowned. Suddenly, there were unexplained shadows everywhere. Agrawal shivered. He looked up and saw a clear sky. Perplexed he turned and scanned the hill and let out a few curses. His men appeared to have walked back down the hill. He wondered if they were retreating, leaving him alone here.

A cold fear gripped him. Had he gone with this too far? He waved and shouted for them to stop. He raised both hands to let out a cry.

Then it happened. Fast and Furious.

There was a flash of light, a thunder-like sound and smoke where Agrawal was standing with his hands up in the air. Das and Mohanty stood still looking at the spectacle as their jaws dropped.

The villagers ran back, shouting for help. It lasted for barely a few seconds. Suddenly, there was absolute stillness everywhere, as if nothing had happened.

Das and Mohanty kept shouting for Agrawal to come back and kept calling his name. They heard nothing. Saw nothing.

They waited and decided to return to the hill with a rescue team in the morning.

Agrawal was not to be found. The search went on for two days. They collected stories from the villagers. Various theories floated, ranging from the mundane to the ludicrous. Paranormal activities, ghosts of dead miners were talked about in hushed tones. Not to mention matters like women getting possessed by the spirits.

The rescue team returned to the city. The team's preliminary observation was that Agrawal must have accidentally stepped on a land mine someone must have illegally planted to keep poachers away, and it must have gone off. Since the top of the hill consisted of soft soil, it was possible that it opened up and took him in without a trace.

It strongly noted that the victim had deliberately violated all safety norms and repeated warnings from the villagers and was himself responsible for the disaster. The search was discontinued, and the case closed.

• • •

It was mid-April, and summer had commenced. The plane from Mumbai landed in Bhubaneswar on time.

Amongst the passengers was a Chinese man in a grey suit. He quickly disembarked and moved towards the exit. As he came out wiping his face and squinting at the bright sunlight outside, he heard a voice.

"Good morning, Mr Han. Welcome to Odisha. I have come to take you to the fantastic iron ore mine."

It was Mohanty.

The End

Horror on the Beach

A tiny coastal town tucked away in the Konkan region of Maharashtra, Alibag is a trendy weekend getaway/ holiday destination, especially for people in Mumbai. It has earned itself the name of 'mini-Goa', owing to the high tourist footfall.

Steeped in colonial history, Alibag is a quaint little town located about 110 kilometres from Mumbai and is replete with sandy beaches, clean unpolluted air and plenty of forts and temples, not to mention the beach that is famously known for an innumerable number of movie shootings.

• • •

In December, it was a long weekend when Alex Kuruvilla and Amir Rana decided to unwind at Alibag.

While they came from entirely different backgrounds, they had their love for the outdoors in common.

It was a stressful week in the office, trying to meet the deadlines. They worked in different companies and met at a well-known place during lunch breaks. Though they took some time to become friends, they eventually toasted to their friendship during the 'Happy Hours'. It was a 'buddy thing'.

They decided to take a catamaran from the Gateway of India to the nearest Mandwa jetty. The trip took about 45 minutes, and buses waited there to take them to Alibag. The beach was a walking distance from the bus stop.

They checked into an old beach house. The caretaker greeted Alex, "Good to see you again, Sir. How are you? How is your wife?"

Alex gave him a perplexed look. "Sorry. I have never come here before, and I'm not married."

"I apologize, Sir!" The caretaker offered a rueful look." I mistook you for somebody else."

He told them that a young girl had taken the room they had booked the previous night, and they had to share a room.

"Not to worry, Sir," he reassured them. "It has all the modern-day facilities. I guarantee you'll like it. It is better than the room you took last time."

Alex looked perplexed. He again reminded Rana that he must have mistaken him for someone else and that this was his first visit.

They decided to explore the sand beds and some local watering holes for a beer late in the evening. They trekked through the dried sand bed; they noticed human, canine, and feline footprints in the mud.

Alex called out to Rana suddenly. "I feel an odd sensation like we are being watched."

A few feet away, Rana motioned frantically and pointed his fingers to a lump of wet sand near him. There was a bone in the ground. At first, they thought it was a bone of some animal. They continued looking around the sand bed when they found a strange blue coloured object sticking out from the sand. When they got closer, they realized it was ladies' beach footwear. Alex bent down to pick it up for closer examination.

"No! Don't do it!" a girl's voice begged. "Go back," Alex looked around but didn't see anyone besides themselves.

"What happened? Why did you stop suddenly?" Rana queried.

"Didn't you hear the girl?" Alex replied, spreading his hands wide. Both confused, they decided to shrug it off and continued on their way. Meanwhile, the feeling that someone was watching them grew more assertive. A few minutes later, they spotted another bone.

Now, they began to get scared. The bone was human.

They quickly retraced their steps and headed backed to their nearby beach house.

• • •

That night, they stayed up binge-watching movies on TV. It was about 2 a.m. when they turned the lights off and called it a night. That was when they heard three light knocks outside their door. Since a thin wall separated the rooms, they assumed it was the girl in the next room.

"Who is it?" Alex called out but didn't get a response. When they left their room to have breakfast in the morning, he saw an attractive young girl standing at the door.

"Were you comfortable and had a good night's sleep?" Alex enquired in a friendly way. She didn't respond but smiled and nodded her head. Alex said, "I heard someone knocking on our door late last night, and I thought you might be wanting something. But when we checked, there was no one."

"Oh!" said the girl." I heard a knock on my door. I thought you were knocking on my door!"

Alex quickly excused himself and headed in the direction of Rana, who was standing at the gate waiting for him. They decided to go shopping and made their way into town and went on a binge.

"Do you have a girlfriend?" Rana blurted. They were into their third drink and were feeling a bit tipsy. Alex lifted his head from the glass he held and glanced at him.

After a few moments, he said, "I did have a girlfriend. That was four years ago. Forget it!"

Rana prodded him. "Come on, tell me all about her. Your romantic moments. From the moment we arrived here, you seem to have been lost in her thoughts."

One more stiff drink loosened Alex. He seemed to drop his inhibitions.

"I met Anita at a common friend's birthday party," he started in a sombre tone. "She had just arrived from Delhi and had landed a plum post in a leading ad agency. She was alone in the city. She was popular, fun and pretty.

We started going out on dates, although there were things about the complex relationship. Soon she moved into my apartment, and things began to change."

"She didn't like me going out without her. She became very possessive and quarrelsome. Arguments became more regular, often physical. I couldn't take it any longer. Soon we broke up on a bitter note, and she said she was going back to Delhi. She even demanded a considerable sum of money. That was four years ago, and I am trying hard to forget the bitter relationship."

"I am sorry to hear that," Rana sympathized with Alex.

"Past is past. Forget it. Let's get back to our nest. It is already late."

• • •

Soon, they were back in their room in the beach house. Alex stared at the blank wall of his room. Rana had stepped out to get some fresh air and clear his head. But Alex was too drunk to bring himself to do anything. He hated the room. The furniture was old and was creaking. As if this was not enough, the girl next door was on his mind giving him uneasy feelings.

'Let me relax as much as possible before returning to my routine and duties. To hell with the girl.' He brushed aside his disturbing thoughts.

The only other thing in the room that was out of place was Rana's old classic sturdy leather travel backpack. And a duffel bag full of his bare necessities and some books. Alex glanced around and surreptitiously opened the leather bag.

Tucked away in an inside pocket of the bag was a butcher's knife, a killer's specialized weapon. The knife Rana had purchased in the morning in a shady market. A bit too slick, Alex thought as he slid his finger along the edge of the blade. He told Alex in a relatively smooth tone that they were in a remote place and had to take care of themselves.

That's when he heard three knocks on the door. Alex opened the door to his room and practically fell into the veranda. Suddenly he felt a presence, and he turned to see the girl next door standing right in front of her room. "You need to be stronger than this, Alex," she said. Her eyes seemed icy and different, almost the opposite of the person he saw that morning. "You have to catch my killer. When I died, they gave me a choice. I chose to come back to help you, but I can't do much."

Her eyes bore into Alex. "You will take care of my killer, won't you?" her voice became slightly deeper.

'It doesn't matter,' Alex mumbled to himself. 'You're a hallucination; get out of my head.'

"If you want to believe that, then give up, Alex," the girl said, sweetness, drained out of her voice. Alex realized that she was challenging him.

"Go to the police station and check with Inspector Sawant. If he doesn't know anything about the murder, then you know I'm not real..."the girl's voice trailed off.

Alex heard the sound of footsteps outside, and he quickly turned to see Rana walking in.

"What are you up to?"

"I was just," Alex turned around, but the girl vanished into thin air. "Never mind," Alex growled, stumbling back into the room.

"I think you need to eat your dinner to feel better. You are drunk and high. I'll come with you," Rana said as he pulled Alex out of his bed. "I haven't eaten too. Let's go."

"Fine," Alex grumbled, walking past him. When the pair finished a hearty dinner, they walked the small path up to the sidewalk. Rana, being quicker, was walking ahead of him.

The road was silent that night, making everything a little eerie. The fact that Alex was following a lead given to him by the girl next door wasn't making him feel good. The shadows seemed particularly dark tonight, almost as if they were preparing to leap out at him.

Every street lamp they passed seemed to be dead. In the absence of light, the entire scene looked gloomy. Now Alex wasn't entirely happy for Rana's pushiness to go out for dinner at this later hour.

He began to shiver a little. The cold December breeze sneaking its way was unforgiving.

Suddenly, Alex felt an icy breeze, the coldest he had felt yet when a dark shape passed by him. Alex stopped abruptly; he was surprised and stumbled. He managed to keep his balance as his knees connected with the hard pavement. He stood up, embarrassed, with aching knees. He squinted into the shadows of the alley but saw nothing.

"Maybe it was just a bat," Rana said softly, quickly coming back to give him a hand. Alex shook his head. It had been far too big to be a bat.

"I would like to walk faster," said Rana, and he moved ahead without waiting for Alex to react.

"I'm sorry. I didn't mean to startle you," said a soft voice in the shadows, light and familiar.

"Stay back," Alex said menacingly. He stepped forward, and the girl stuck her arm out in front of him. Alex squinted his eyes in her direction, trying to make out her features.

A few seconds passed before the girl stepped out of the shadows. She looked the same, except now her dress was in tatters, torn all over.

"What can I tell you? A girl has decided to avenge her killing, "the girl spoke in a tone that showed no emotion. Alex was about to say something when the girl began speaking again.

"You killed her. You watched her die," the girl watched in his direction with a vacant expression.

"That is why she will not allow you to kill her brother too. He is the only member in the family now."

Fire blazed in front of Alex's eyes before she disappeared without a trace.

Alex called out for Rana, his head swimming. He didn't find him and started staggering back to his cottage.

About a half-hour later, he reached the cabin alone. Rana was missing. He went outside to look for him when he noticed a figure staring in the direction of the beach.

When he turned, Alex could see Rana with a grim expression.

"Alex? You are back. Come with me. Let's take a walk on the beach." His eyes bore deep into Alex. Silently he began to walk towards the beach.

Rana walked ahead on the beach, and Alex followed. His mind was blank, and he felt as though he was drugged.

Rana suddenly stopped and turned, handing Alex the butcher's knife. "I bought it this morning. It comes in handy when cutting a body to pieces. Isn't it?"

He then turned and continued walking. Alex tucked the knife under his sweater and followed.

When they reached where they had found the bone, Rana went deep into the shadows, leaving Alex standing alone. Then, suddenly, Rana burst out of the dark shadows in front of Alex. Alex was terrified.

"You killed my sister, the only person I loved on the earth. After my parents met with an untimely death in a car accident, she was everything in my life. I loved her very much. Everyone loved her and her helpful nature. You were jealous of her and started living off her earnings. And soon you started cheating on her. You picked quarrels with her. In the guise of marrying her, you brought her here. But instead, you murdered her on this deserted beach."

Alex was too shocked to utter a single word of protest.

"You had bought a butcher's knife from the same shop I bought it, cut her to pieces and buried her at different places. You managed to disappear the same night under cover of darkness."

Rana choked with sadness and rage. "And now it is time for you to die," he hissed.

Alex grinned and took out the butcher's knife Rana had given him.

"You were foolish enough to trust me and give me the knife, Rana. It is your turn to die and join your sister."

Alex leapt forward with the butcher's knife held firmly in his hand. But he was flung into the air by an unknown force and fell a few feet away.

He groped the sand to pick himself up but didn't let go of the butcher's knife. His fingers grazed a strange object and he picked it up from the sand. It was a human skull. He thought it was a stone he could hit Rana with. He let out a cry and threw the skull away.

With difficulty, he got up and went to Rana again. He felt a strong force was holding him back and was snatching the knife from him. Unable to bear the pain, he let go of the blade.

Rana was slowly coming towards him. Looking Alex in the eye, he bent down and picked up the butcher's knife.

Alex felt he watched a movie in slow motion and could not move.

Then he saw a figure next to Rana. It first appeared shapeless. And to his horror, Alex saw the distorted figure turning into Anita. She had appeared beside her brother.

Alex sprung forward to catch the butcher's knife. But he was too late.

The butcher's knife had found its mark.

The End

Final Destination

The invitation read:

Join Us

for a

Happy Halloween Thriller Bash

Hosted by the Adam's Family

Oct 31, 6 PM

'Shortcut to Heaven', Spooky Road,

RSVP: 1313-1313-1313

Wear your spookiest costume.

I stirred behind my closed eyelids, my mind ceasing to be in the dream mode to bring me back to wakefulness. At first, I was confused. A slow smile crept over my face. I realized I was drinking till the wee hours of the morning.

I had drawn the curtains tightly to get undisturbed sleep till late hours in the morning. I rolled to get up as my eyes opened to see the rainfall, already feeling the soothing coldness of the breeze.

There was the scent of wetness, so ever-present in the autumn. Today will be a day to enjoy all the things that go with a change in season.

Outside was an unexpected gift of rain. The wet season didn't generally start for another fortnight, but the skies don't lie. It wasn't a mean rain either, the type that got everyone wet.

The rain had fallen steadily without letting up since early, even before I had woken up. Outside, the autumn leaves drooped under the weight of the droplets.

Suddenly I felt hungry. The sight and aroma of the food was a gentle massage to my soul. Then I got ready for the Halloween party.

It was still early when the clouds gave their rain to the grass and trees when the road became alive with more splashes than my eyes could appreciate. Something about this rain had me more relaxed than in days, and I was in no hurry for the clouds to vanish.

The cars moved past steadily. The traffic snaked up the hill, two lines of steel and tyre. It got dark quickly. I drove steadily and felt I was going through space in dreamy awe.

There was plenty of time to take it easy upon the journey with the car on autopilot and the motor in splendid electric silence. Fresh air flowed into the car, bringing the freshness of the country air to my senses.

The mist danced upon the wet road as if it were in some magical daydream. The car hugged the black tarmac, bright headlamps illuminating the road onward.

One moment the road was there, wide open and safe; the next, there were loud noises, acrid smells and pain that you may or may not recover from. The car crash came as a shock, a form of emotional blindness.

From the mangled metal, I extricated myself. My car wheels had turned over the wet track—belly up.

• • •

The cold rain rammed into my face harder, and I walked away. Then, to my surprise, what I heard was my laughter. I found myself so deeply funny standing at the edge of the road in my Halloween costume, looking scarier than a ghoul.

Then, head down, I started walking, thinking of the warmth at the home of Adam's family.

It was close to midnight.

From a distance, I could have sworn I saw the entire haunted house bend into some Halloween smile as October 31st came closer – as if the spirit of the house needed to grin, welcoming me.

Soon, I was relieved to see the Adam Family's Mansion, 'Shortcut to Heaven'. It looked like a haunted house. I didn't see smoke from its chimney or lights through the broken window panes.

As I approached the house, the Halloween decorations shone white, echoing the starlit night and the moon's beauty. I wondered how the inclement weather could change into a glorious night in such a short period.

Halloween decorations called out to the night with a steady golden glow.

As I entered the Halloween house, I noticed that it was less of a Halloween party and more of a Zombie Halloween ball, from flowing ghoul-gowns to eyeball Halloween treats and candy-floss cobwebs.

"We are happy you could make it," a lady I thought was the hostess, welcomed me at the entrance. She was gorgeous, looking like a Hollywood star.

"Thank you," I replied politely. "It is very kind of you to invite me. I am honoured."

It looked like a family-friendly Halloween party on one side of the large hall. There were cute monsters and pumpkin Cheshire smiles.

When my hostess flowed in dance, it was as if it were the only way her body truly knew how to speak. For the most part, she was fascinated by that old music machine.

She looked so familiar to me. As I turned, her eyes caught me staring at her. I dropped my eyes momentarily, and a hopeful smile played on my lips.

I asked her hesitatingly. "Pardon my curiosity. Aren't you Marylyn Monroe, yesteryear's popular movie star? My granddad was in awe of you. I have watched the reruns of your movies on TV along with him."

My sexy hostess smiled and moved on. She never walked anywhere. Her legs extended like a prima ballerina, and she glided from place to place, arms held in front, fingertips touching. Watching her was breathtaking. For her, a moment spent not dancing was a moment wasted.

I went near a large window and looked outside. The mist danced upon the garden as if it were in some magical daydream. It was like black space that carries the light, that allows us to see the guiding stars.

Outside was an unexpected gift of rain. Yet together, they brought such a soothing sound, a natural melody every bit as beautiful as a mother's soulful hums.

Puzzled, I stepped out and felt each splash that touched my skin.

I watched in amazement. My Halloween costume was not getting wet. My skin was as dry as dust.

Suddenly, one by one, the guests started removing the masks. They all looked familiar to me; musicians, actors, sports personalities, poets and the like. I thought I recognized Shakespeare, Leonardo da Vinci, Michelangelo, Beethoven!

At the centre of the huge hall, I saw Michael Jackson grooving to raucous music with a horde of dancers. My jaw dropped.

Then I saw a mysterious figure walking towards me. I was alarmed. The man was wearing what looked like an iron mask. But who was he? I wondered. The man in the iron mask came near me and removed his mask.

"Have you already forgotten me, my dear young man? I'm your grandfather. I died only a year ago."

I gaped at him, jaws dropping.

"Don't worry," he smiled consolingly. "Join MJ's Thriller in the dance of the Undead."

Then it started falling in place.

I was no longer a guest. I had become one of them. I can now meet God with full pride, I can return the smiling gaze of our creator, and so now I am finally happy.

The Thriller had reached the climax.

Then suddenly, the ear-splitting music started, and I saw Michael Jackson grooving with a horde of the Undead, just like in the video 'Thriller'. He was making his well-known moves of Crotch Grab, anti-gravity lean and the MJ Spin.

I was thrilled.

The End